The BOUNCER

David Gordon holds an MA in English and Comparative Literature and an MFA in Writing from Columbia University. His work has appeared in the *Paris Review*, the *New York Times* and the *Los Angeles Review of Books*.

Also by David Gordon

White Tiger on Snow Mountain: Stories
Mystery Girl
The Serialist

The BOUNCER

DAVID GORDON

Leabharlanna Poiblí Chathair Baile Átha Cliath
Dublin City Public Libraries

A Mysterious Press book for
Head of Zeus

First published in the US in 2018 by Mysterious Press,
an imprint of Grove/Atlantic, New York

First published in the UK in 2018 by Head of Zeus

9 7 5 3 1 2 4 6 8

A catalogue record for this book is available from the British Library.

ISBN (HB): 9781788543767
ISBN (TPB): 9781788543774
ISBN (E): 9781788543750

This book was set in 12 pt. Adobe Garamond Pro by
Alpha Design & Composition of Pittsfield, NH.

Printed and bound by CPI Group (UK) Ltd, Croydon, CR0 4YY

Head of Zeus Ltd
First Floor East
5–8 Hardwick Street
London EC1R 4RG
WWW.HEADOFZEUS.COM

For my family and friends

Part I

1

When the drunken football player went berserk and tried to steal a stripper, everyone yelled to get the bouncer. This drunk was huge, a redheaded giant. He lunged for the stage, grabbing and squeezing like a starving caveman at an all-you-can-eat buffet, then went straight for Kimberly, a tall blonde curved like a futurist Italian sculpture. He snatched her right off the stage, tossing her over his shoulder like King Kong. When a waitress protested, he swatted her away like a fly. The bartender, a buffed-up dude who CrossFit like crazy, punched him right in the gut. The giant just kind of blinked, as if he'd been distracted for a second by a passing thought, then creamed the bartender with one blow. Even when his own friends tried to take him down, he sent them flying, drunk out of his mind, screaming, "I don't wanna get married!" It was a bachelor party gone very wrong.

So Crystal, a new girl who had just moved to New York from Philly, ran off to find the bouncer, Joe, who was on a break, sitting in a back booth, drinking coffee and reading a fat, dog-eared copy of Dostoyevsky's *The Idiot*. At first glance she was not impressed. He was cute, if you liked tall, lean, scruffy white boys, which she occasionally did, but as muscle he wasn't much compared to the human mountains in black suits she was used to seeing at the doors of clubs. This guy was in jeans and old Converse high-tops, wearing a T-shirt that said SECURITY, but the giant was about four times his size. If the giant were a tree and you sawed him in half, then filled him with steaming bubbles, Joe and Crystal could both sit in his hollow trunk as if they were in a hot tub.

"Hey, you!" she shouted. "The idiot! We need help!"

Joe looked up, sort of smiling mildly, and folded the page of his book. Then he saw where Crystal was pointing. The giant was wading through the crowd, apparently hauling Kim off to his lair to eat later. Moving easy, Joe stepped right into his path.

"Hey! You! Meat!" he yelled. "Over here."

The giant made a frowny face, focusing on Joe like a bull seeing a red flag. "Don't call me that."

Joe grinned. "How about I give you a lap dance?"

Grumbling, the giant tossed Kim to the side, and she crashed onto a table of Asian tourists. Then he made for Joe. Crystal felt a little bad as she braced herself to watch that pretty face get ugly. The giant hauled off and threw a punch, his fist coming down like a sledgehammer. But Joe dipped gracefully and, riding on the balls of his feet, stepped safely inside the swing. He kicked out, knocking the giant's shin from under him. As he stumbled, Joe reached in to grab a point on his thick neck.

"Ow!" Like a wounded monster, the giant howled in pain and tried to shake loose, but Joe just pinched harder.

"Easy, easy, let's walk," he said, leading the bent giant along, groaning and moaning. The crowd parted and they went right out the door.

Kimberly got up, slowly, with the help of the tourists.

"Wow," she said to Crystal. "Now that's a good bouncer."

Crystal nodded. "I guess it pays to read up on idiots."

2

Outside, on the steps of Club Rendezvous—QUEENS' FINEST
GENTLEMAN'S CLUB, CONVENIENTLY CLOSE TO THE AIRPORT—
Joe and the giant now sat side by side. It was a warm summer
night. The air felt soft and fresh, as if it had been trucked
in from the country, and the planes overhead could almost
have been comets. The giant was crying. His name, by the
way, was Jerry, and now that he had crumpled, slumped over
and sniffling, while Joe patted his back, he looked more like
a huge pink baby than anything else. And like a baby he
was sweet and not too bright, and capable of causing great
damage without really meaning it.

"I don't know what happens when I drink," Jerry the giant
baby said, wiping his nose. "I lose all control. I'm not a bad
guy. I love my fiancée."

Joe nodded. "I know, man. I've been there, believe me.
Don't be afraid to reach out for help if you need it."

Jerry looked over, tears shining in the neon. "Are you
ever afraid, Joe?"

Joe laughed a short, hard laugh. "Jerry, I wake up in terror
every damn day."

"Really? What could you be afraid of?"

Joe paused for a moment, considering. He scratched his chin, staring up at a plane that, unbeknownst to him, was bound for Venice. He smiled and turned back to Jerry. Then the law arrived.

Really the law descended. All at once they were there, from all sides, guns drawn. It was a full-on assault, SWAT in body armor coming around the building, grunting and barking orders; black SUVs full of Feds pulling up like clown cars and haircuts spilling out; NYPD uniforms screeching in to block traffic and secure the parking lot, like the overpriced security guards they often were.

"Hey, hey, take it easy," Joe said, calm but loud, hands raised but very still otherwise. "Everything's cool. We're unarmed."

Really terrified now, Jerry looked at Joe and then raised his arms as well.

SWAT moved in, patting them down, still grunting. "Clear!"

The sirens, though silenced, still throbbed redly, and the headlights peeled back the shadows to expose Joe and Jerry in the white glare. They blinked in blind confusion.

"We're okay," Joe called out. "False alarm. We don't need any help." Joe didn't know who called the cops, but it had to be some citizen freaked out by the fight. This was Gio's place. Gio's kind of people do not call the cops. They call Joe.

Agent Donna Zamora stepped up. She was in a windbreaker marked FBI, with her hair up under a cap, also marked FBI, and with her badge on her belt—basically an outfit that says, *Don't accidentally shoot me,* but still she somehow made it look good.

"Thanks for coming," Joe said. "But we're doing much better now."

"That's nice to hear," she said, amused. She holstered her gun.

Joe smiled, and she noticed he had nice eyes, also somehow amused, though it was hard to say at what.

"Yeah," he went on. "It was just a misunderstanding. We don't need your help after all."

Now she had to laugh. "You're right. There is a misunderstanding." She held up her cuffs. "We're not here to help you. We're here to place you under arrest."

And as he stood, helping Jerry up and turning around to let her cuff him, she heard him laughing, too.

3

The phone woke Gio. It was his cell, his work phone, a disposable he changed frequently, not that he said anything that mattered on the phone, but it was still smart to keep it separate from the phone he used to call his wife, text his kids, take pictures of fish they caught on his boat. Nor was it the landline, which basically just his relatives and in-laws used, and at this time of night—Jesus, it said two fucking A.M. on his bedside clock—would have to mean somebody dead or in the hospital. Carol groaned beside him.

"Whazzut?"

"Nothing, baby, go back to sleep. Just work," Gio said, patting her shoulder and carrying the phone swiftly into the master bath. She would be up in four hours to meditate and do her Pilates before waking the kids. He shut the door carefully behind him and sat on the toilet lid. The marble tiles chilled his feet.

"What?"

The voice was Fusco's. "It's me. We need to talk."

"Now?"

"The sooner the better."

"I'm on my way. See you there."

He pressed the red button and made a mental note to toss the phone as soon as he was away from the house.

Gio was a gangster. A mobster. A third-generation high-ranking professional in the field of organized crime. But if you saw him, or met him, or spent time at his home in a leafy, quiet part of Long Island, on a big parcel of land—a huge but very tasteful white shingle house with an immense lawn, an organic vegetable garden, and a pool—you would never think it in a million years. Carol, his wife, was a child psychologist with her own practice now that the kids were getting big. His kids were typical American kids in all the good and bad ways that implied—cute, smart, dumb, happy, lazy, spoiled, lovable. Their idea of a gangster came from rap videos, and the only person his son wanted to whack was his math teacher. They thought Gio ran the family business, which he did, but they knew only about the legitimate half: a sprawling real estate empire, mainly commercial but including some apartment buildings in Brooklyn and Queens that had become very valuable lately; a heavyweight investment portfolio comprising a wide range of blue chips, tech funds, foreign investments, bonds, even some chunks in hedge funds and venture capital; a highway and road paving company, a trucking company, and a general contracting business, all run by cousins and nieces and nephews, under his oversight; and a few old family legacies, like the seafood restaurant that all the kids had to work at during the summers and that they all hated—that he, too, had hated when he worked there, boiling shrimp and wiping up red sauce—and that was worth more for the waterfront land it stood on than anything else, but that his widowed mother would kill him over if he ever sold it or changed one Sinatra picture on the wall. Her grandfather had started it when he arrived in America. Giovanni was named for him.

Another reason you would not think of Gio as a gangster is that he had worked hard to achieve the appearance of an upstanding citizen. He'd been to college and business school, even interning on Wall Street. He had, since he stepped up, shifted his family's focus from the old and still vibrant world of gambling, sex, extortion, and loan-sharking to more contemporary and less colorful crimes, like Internet credit card fraud, stock manipulation, and money laundering. He wore suits from Brooks Brothers, not silks from Little Italy. He drove an Audi. He played golf with doctors and judges. He even went vegetarian for a couple of weeks once when his cholesterol spiked and his wife freaked.

But Gio was still a gangster. And when he drove out to the Parkview Diner to meet NYPD detective Jimmy Fusco, the compulsive gambler who fed him information in the hope of paying down his constantly growing debt, and learned that his club had been raided because someone had reported the hand jobs that were occasionally on sale in the VIP lounge, his first thought was: *I will find the fucking rat who dimed me and pull his goddamn tongue out through the gaping hole I slice in his throat.* Not to mention the money he paid out monthly in bribes.

"What the fuck, Jimmy?" he asked Fusco as they sat in the idling Audi, in the back behind the diner, with Fusco's city-issued Chevy parked nearby. "I'm supposed to be immune to this shit, the money I spend."

Fusco shrugged nervously. He was dying for a smoke but knew that wasn't allowed in Gio's car. "It's not my fault, Gio. I swear. There's nothing I can do. It's federal. You know, because of ices."

Gio made a face, head shaking. "Ices? My trucks? This is about Italian fucking ices and soft serve? Okay, they sell some weed and maybe a little coke off the trucks"—he held a finger up—"but never to kids and never near schools. I'm adamant about that."

"No, Gio." Fusco spelled it: "I-S-I-S. You know, terrorism. The whole city is on high alert." He saw outrage in Gio's eyes and shrank back in his seat, though there was nowhere to go.

Gio's voice was flat. "You think I'm a terrorist? You think I have anything to do with those pieces of shit?"

"No! Never. Of course not." Fusco waved his hand, as though trying to cool Gio off. "And neither do the Feds, really. It's not like you specifically. They're cracking down on everybody." He took a breath. "I mean, you're the furthest thing from a terrorist, we both know that, but with all due respect . . . what about illegal gun sales? Drug profits going all over the world? Money laundering? Illegals being smuggled in? Undocumented sex workers?" He winced again, fearing another outburst. "Look, it's a new world. They have intel on known terror suspects planning something in New York. And until the fear level subsides, or the cops and Feds get some results, everyone—you, me, everybody—is going to be under pressure." Fusco sighed and reflexively put a cigarette in his mouth. "And like it or not, people talk under pressure."

"Don't light that in here."

"No." He took it out of his mouth. "I wouldn't."

Gio took a breath. He was calm again. Thoughtful. "So," he said, now with a tight little smile, "who talked about my club?"

4

In lockup, Joe was making the best of it, sitting on a bench, chatting with his new pal Jerry and the other, more familiar faces in the overcrowded holding cell. They were packed in like commuters on a rush-hour express, but with a stainless steel toilet in the middle. It seemed like everybody got busted tonight: a Chinese betting parlor, a Russian brothel, a crack house in the Bronx, a chop shop run by Dominicans uptown, a warehouse of stolen goods—jewelry, cameras, and other electronics—handled by guys in yarmulkes in Crown Heights. Everyone was swarmed with cops and Feds, then led away in cuffs, loaded onto buses, laboriously processed, and dumped behind bars to wait. The whole town was here. It was like a class reunion for organized crime.

And everyone said the same thing: *The heat was on.* Every kind of law—federal, local, state—was cracking down on every sector of the New York underworld, trying to flush out hidden bogeymen. Which they were not going to find. It was a monumental waste of time. Everyone in the cell knew that, and so did everyone outside the cell, at least up to the rank of captain. But until they satisfied the media and the politicians that they were serious, and calmed the panicked populace; until the taxpayers and voters—neither a group much represented in here—stopped seeing suicide bombers under their beds and the world's attention moved on to something else, nobody was getting any business done. In other words, Joe was out of a job.

Jerry was nervous. "Joe, I've never been arrested before. You know, pulled over a couple times, but never like this." He scanned the crowd. "Are all these guys criminals?"

"As far as I know," Joe said. "But don't worry. Just stick close to me. I made a call. We'll be out . . ." He hesitated, not wanting to promise too much. ". . . eventually."

Then Derek squeezed by. "Hey, Joe!"

"Hi, Derek." They shook hands. Joe liked Derek, a Chinese kid from Flushing. He was young, twenty-one or -two at the most, but unlike a lot of the young dudes, he wasn't fixated on either impressing you or snarling if you seemed unimpressed, a routine that Joe found exhausting. Derek had a positive attitude. He was more like a cheerful go-getter, an eager up-and-coming professional. His profession was thief.

Joe gestured at the packed bench. Ten guys butt-to-butt. "I'd say have a seat, but it would need to be on my lap."

Derek grinned. "That's okay. I'll let you elders sit, like on the bus." He looked around. "This is some shitshow, though, right?"

"That's the word I'd pick."

"Three of my uncle's places got shut down. Man, is he pissed off."

"Rightfully so."

Derek's uncle ran numerous gambling parlors in the Chinese parts of town. He also shipped stolen cars, jewelry, and antiques to mainland China via the black market, a substantial percentage of which Derek stole.

Derek crouched down and asked in a quieter voice, "Who's this?" nodding his chin at Jerry.

"Just a guy from the club. He's okay."

Derek leaned in closer. "Look, seeing as you're going to be out of work like me, I thought I'd tell you about a little something I could let you in on."

Joe nodded, just a fraction of an inch, but enough for Derek to continue: "It's a heist. A contract job. The plan, the client, everything is set up. We just need one more man."

"To do what?"

Derek grinned. "I know you don't like the heavy stuff, so you can drive." He punched Joe's arm lightly. "You're one of the few I'd trust behind the wheel."

Joe laughed. "Thanks, but I don't know. Like you said, I'm old and lazy. This sounds . . ." He shrugged. ". . . exciting."

"I know, I know. Cowboys and Indians. Or native peoples or whatever the fuck. But I've got to earn. I'm getting married in a month."

"Really? Congratulations. So is Jerry over here."

"No shit?" Derek sighed. "Man, I love this girl, but to be honest, I'm kind of losing it."

Joe stood up and gave Derek his seat. "So is Jerry. You two should talk."

* * *

It was well into the next day when Joe got out. Gio's lawyer sprang him and the other club employees. Jerry and Derek were helped by the relatives or friends they'd called. By the time they got reprocessed all over again, and walked out of the detention center and onto Baxter Street as free men, it was lunchtime. Enough time for Jerry and Derek to bond and for Jerry to insist that both of them come to his wedding. He hugged them each tightly and ran off. His dad was double-parked and angrily honking. Derek made a quieter exit, slipping off to a white BMW purring up the block. Joe was thinking about getting an iced coffee from one of the Vietnamese places across from the Tombs, where he'd been going for pho and crispy squid almost as long as he'd been getting arrested: strong black coffee dripped onto sticky, sweet condensed milk and then poured onto ice. Then he saw that cute Fed from last night. She was standing to the side, wearing shades, watching the parade of arrestees go by. She was dressed in a suit now, some kind of silky black fabric over a silky white blouse. It was, well, very FBI. She was a suit after all, but hers was cut to hang and cling quite gracefully on narrow shoulders and the curve of chest and hips. No doubt it cost quite a bit. As did her haircut: her hair was down now and Joe could see it was very long, very shiny, and very black. He didn't realize how black until he saw it in the daylight.

He smiled and gave a little wave, and when she nodded, he walked over.

"Good morning," he said. "Or afternoon."

"You, too," she said, not really looking at him, or at least not turning her head. "Nice night?"

"I've had worse. You?"

"Busy," she said. "I didn't sleep much."

"That's too bad. They don't pay you enough to work so hard."

She looked at him. "Who says I was working?"

Joe laughed. Emboldened, he said, "Hey, how about, just to show there's no hard feelings—want to come with me to a wedding?"

Now she laughed. He'd caught her off guard. "When?"

"Tonight! That's whose bachelor party you raided."

"In that case, I don't know that I'd be welcome."

"Of course you would. Jerry is all heart. And it's going to be a Scottish-Korean wedding. Should be pretty wild."

"That does sound like fun. But I'm busy. Maybe another time." And now she smiled, a real smile, right at him as she turned and went inside. Joe watched her, then saw Crystal and Kimberly among a group of women being released through another door and heading toward a waiting black car.

"Hey, ladies," he called, walking over. "Can you give me a ride?"

5

Agent Donna Zamora was surprised at herself. She'd slipped. She'd let herself be charmed, even found herself flirting before she realized she was doing it, and with a perp, a bouncer from a titty bar who just went by Joe. Even for her pretty much disastrous love life, that was a step down. *Who said I was working?* How could she have said that? It was shameless, she thought, and, if her colleagues had heard, brainless. Then why was she smiling as she recalled him smiling, the look of happy surprise on his face, that air he had of being in on some secret joke? But was the joke with her? On her? On himself?

Anyway, a smile was a smile, and she had to take what she could get, stuck in a dead-end job in a shitty little office, as far from the action as you could be and still wear a gun to work: She was the tip girl. The hotline. And no, that was not as sexy as it sounds. What she did was answer calls all day from loyal citizens who thought their neighbors' trash smelled suspicious and comb through e-mails from watchful civilians who noticed their cabdriver had a Muslimish name, or that someone left a pizza box on the subway, or the loud

party on the roof had Mexican-sounding music. Never mind
that she was part Mexican and part Puerto Rican herself.
Never mind her degree and being the best shot in her class
at Quantico. In the white-bread locker-room culture of the
FBI, Donna was stuck in the dreary job of manning—even
the verb was discriminatory—the tip line, dealing with every
dumb-ass who sees something and says something. Unless
she could make one of the tips pay. That was why, when that
cokehead from Canarsie called about the Middle Eastern
businessmen getting hand jobs from blondes in the VIP
lounge at Club Rendezvous, she strapped up and rode along.
At least it got her out in the field for a night, in the open
air, where she could breathe a little. And maybe even run.

She sighed, glancing up at the photos and sketches of
the top ten faces on the terrorist watch list, faces that stared
at her all day, mocking her, daring her to find them in the
bottomless pile of bullshit she shoveled. She gave them all
the finger. She killed her cold coffee and got ready to return
another pointless call when the phone rang. It was her direct
extension, most likely another small-time sleazebag or paranoid schizophrenic looking for reward money. She picked up.

"Good afternoon, this is Agent Zamora, do you have a
crime to report?"

"Hi," a friendly, non-sleazy, non-schizo voice said. "My
name is Giovanni Caprisi. I want to come by and talk."

Giovanni fucking Caprisi. Gio the Gent. Coming by. In
the flesh. To talk. Holy shit. Donna laughed out loud. She'd
won the lottery. A major OC target. The head of a goddamn
Mafia crime family, coming in of his own free will. Who
knows what he wanted or whom he was ready to give up?

Maybe he was looking to tip her off about a competitor or a rival from within his family. Maybe he was ready to chuck it in, turn state's evidence, and go into witness protection. If it broke right, it could be a career-making case. For sure it would get her off the tip line.

So she told him yes, absolutely, come right over. She called and left his name downstairs. Then she ran to the restroom, got her look together, and came back to wait calmly until she got the knock on the door.

"Agent Zamora, your guest is here," the young agent, a crew-cut boy in a blazer, said.

"Thanks. Send him in."

The boy held the door. And there, in a really lovely tan summer suit, with a white shirt and a blue tie, with polished shoes and a Rolex but no gold or rings besides his wedding band, was Gio. He smiled.

"Agent Zamora? It's a pleasure to meet you."

"And you, Mr. Caprisi."

They shook.

"Please call me Gio." He looked around the tiny window-less room. "I'm in the right place? This is where I come to cooperate?"

"Absolutely," she said, moving a stack of useless files from a chair. "Please sit down. And let me assure you that whatever you need from us in exchange for your cooperation, I can get it for you."

"Great. I was hoping you'd say that." He brushed the seat off and sat, hitching his trousers.

"If you need protection for your family, a new identity, even a new face—it's no problem."

"A new face!" He laughed and stroked his chin. "What's wrong with this one? I just had it shaved. You don't like it?"

"No, it's . . . a very nice face. And a very nice close shave, too. I mean, in exchange for your testimony. If you decide to turn state's witness against your associates in organized crime."

Gio laughed harder. "I'm sorry." He caught his breath. "I'm afraid you've got me confused with someone else. I'm just here as a concerned citizen. I know nothing about organized crime. Sounds like an oxymoron to me."

She sat down, sinking into her chair as her hopes sank, too. "Then what do you want to talk to me about?"

"Terrorism."

"What about terrorism?"

"I think it's horrible. It has to be stopped."

"Yes. We here at the FBI agree."

"Good. I'm glad to hear that. And I want to help."

"I'm sorry, Mr. . . . Gio. I don't follow. How can you help?"

"Well, as I mentioned, I'm a concerned citizen, and in the course of my ordinary activities I meet a lot of people and learn a lot of things. Some of them just might be people you're interested in. And at the same time, I also know other people, friends of mine, other loyal citizens, whose businesses are being . . . interfered with by friends of yours."

"You mean like your club?"

"Club Rendezvous? That's not mine. That club happens to be owned by my cousin's wife's neighbor."

"That's right," Donna said. "I forgot. Yettie Greenblatt. The eighty-two-year-old strip club owner."

"Exactly. Poor lady. Her husband's gone. That club is all she has. So let's say I was able to give you, like, one of these guys up here." He nodded at the grim men on the wall, none quite as well shaven as he. "Maybe you'd turn around and help Mrs. Greenblatt with her club."

"Do you have information about a wanted terrorist?"

"Right this moment? No. But I could help look. I could organize, like, a volunteer search party for you. You know, like a deputy. You guys deputize people."

"No. Actually, to my knowledge, we don't. And even if we could, I'm not going to deputize a gangster and turn him loose to hunt for terrorists in exchange for complicity in his illegal activities."

"Whoa. Easy!" Gio laughed, putting his hands up. "You're making it sound much bigger than it is. I was just thinking out loud. How about this? Just as a hypothetical. A thought experiment."

"A thought experiment?"

"Let's say someone anonymously called you and hypothetically helped you catch some of these guys. Would that make life easier for people like Mrs. Greenblatt?"

"Hypothetically?"

"Purely."

She sighed. "Yes, I suppose it would."

"Great," Gio said, jumping up and shaking her hand. "Thanks so much for your time. And if I see any of these fellows, you're the first one I'm going to call."

He left, shutting the door softly behind him. A second later, she burst out laughing. What a joke. At least she hadn't told anybody about her big case. Anyway, it broke up the day. She'd tell her mom about it later, when she stopped by to pick up her kid, and her mom would laugh with her again. She was still chuckling when her phone rang and she picked up.

"Agent Zamora?"

It was her NYPD liaison.

"Yes. Hi. Sorry, I was just clearing my throat. What's up?"

"I've got news on that missing person you asked about? One Billy Rio?"

"Yes?"

Billy Rio was the cokehead from Canarsie. The one who'd dropped a dime on Gio's—or Mrs. Greenblatt's—club. He hadn't shown up to get his reward money—very un-cokehead behavior. And his phone was dead. And his mom, whose basement he lived in, hadn't seen him. So Donna had asked the locals to keep an eye out.

"Yeah, my snitch. What's up?"

"Good news. We found him," the liaison said. "Well, most of him. Anyway, enough to ID."

6

Gio knew that timing was extremely important. He wanted to make an entrance, to show up after all the others had arrived. But he didn't want to keep them waiting too long, either, to bore or bruise any of the overripe egos stuffed into that warehouse, like the place where they stored the Thanksgiving Day parade balloons. And though the security procedures had been exhaustive—the grounds and the guests swept for bugs, cell phones collected at the door—the likelihood of at least some of his visitors being under surveillance was high and the window of opportunity small. So when his new burner phone rang, signaling that the party was assembled, he had his guy Nero, who was driving, pull right up, and only nodded at the guard by the gate before hurrying in.

At least they didn't need to worry about cameras, he thought, as the heavy steel gate swung shut behind him. This place was vast, a kind of indoor landscape enclosed in corrugated steel. Mountains of rock salt and sand, stories high, sat here waiting for winter, shielded from rain and wind by an arching roof and walls. It was built on a pier.

On three sides was water, where the barges unloaded, ton upon ton, and on the shore side, a fenced-in asphalt lot, where the trucks loaded it back up. Gio walked between these dunes, the sun slowly sinking out there somewhere behind the wall, but its rays leaking in through every crack and seam in the rusted shed—in spots the corrosion was like lace, or a confessor's screen—and falling on the artificial mountain range, illuminating its fractured planes, its grains and crystals, painting it red and gold, throwing long and foreshortened shadows over the narrow valleys. He emerged into a section where snowplows were stored, stacked like gigantic spoons high above him. Behind this barricade, in an open area, folding chairs had been set up around bridge tables. On each table were a bowl of fruit, a bottle of seltzer, a bucket of ice, and an assortment of liquor bottles. Off to one side a kid in a suit and tie stood behind an espresso machine. But at a glance, Gio could see that nothing had been touched, except the ashtrays, anachronistically set out in this raw space filled with dirt.

For the most part, despite some gold on teeth, chains, and fingers, and some rough jailhouse tattoos and colored leather, the twenty or so guests looked like what they were, successful businesspeople gathered for serious business. All but one were men—the exception being Little Maria, a diminutive, cheerful woman who, since her husband died, had ruthlessly run most of the Dominican-controlled heroin trade. If you had a bodega on your corner that seemed to sell nothing but some dusty cans of soup and stale candy, that probably belonged to Maria. In age they ranged from midthirties, like Gio himself and Alonzo, who was there representing the black gangs in Brooklyn, to who knows, like the round and age-less Uncle Chen, who ran Flushing (not the Korean parts), and the ancient, black-clad, white-bearded Hasid Menachem "Rebbe" Stone, who, despite his grandfatherly demeanor, ran the Orthodox underworld with an iron hand.

Gio walked in and took a deep breath as the guests all turned to him. "Good afternoon, and thank you for coming. I can't even say what a great honor it is that you would all make the trip. I also want to thank my cousin Ricky for providing the location." He nodded at Ricky, who beamed. Actually he was not a cousin; he was Gio's cousin's husband's kid, and he was a dimwit, and Gio had given him a low-end easy job looking after a couple of union locals, out of family guilt. The obscurity of this small-time operation was part of what made it safe. "Ricky?" he said again. "Thank you."

Ricky jumped, getting the hint, and hurried off, taking the barista—his son—with him. The kid was a real barista who ran a trendy little café in a Carroll Gardens building the family owned. Gio pulled up a chair and sat down. The others all leaned forward and stared in stony silence.

"We all know why we're here. We're all in the same bind and it's hurting. None of us can get back to business till these terrorists are caught. Problem is, the cops couldn't catch crabs in a whorehouse. Not that anyone here's whores have crabs."

There were some laughs, and the ice was broken.

"Okay, we all know we're fucked. I didn't drive an hour to remind myself of that." That was Alexei, a Russian mob boss from Brighton Beach. He lit another cigarette. "The question is, what can we do about it? You have an answer for that one, Gio?"

"I do. We catch them."

"Who? The crabs?" Everyone laughed again and Alexei grinned, though Gio felt that was kind of milking the joke. But he smiled to be polite.

"We catch the terrorists, my friend."

Alexei paused, staring for a moment. Then he tossed his head back and laughed, bigger than ever. Others joined in. "Gio, you really are crazy," he said. "But I admit you have balls. Catch the terrorists."

"How we going to catch those motherfuckers if the whole damn FBI and CIA can't?" Alonzo asked.

"We're the only ones who can," Gio said. "Not the law. Not the press. Us. The people in this room. We've got the connections, the knowledge, the muscle. We have to, to save our businesses. And not only that. The way I see it, it's our duty. None of us here are saints—except of course you, Maria." She laughed at that and nodded. "But whatever we do, it's just business. Between professionals. Soldiers. But these sick terrorist fucks, they kill women, children. Remember those two in California? They gunned down a bunch of retards, for fuck's sake."

At this several of the guests crossed themselves, and Alexei spit on the ground.

Gio continued: "How dare they put us in with those sick maniacs. We are all proud New Yorkers, patriotic Americans whose families came here from somewhere—Russia, Sicily, the Caribbean, Louisiana—fleeing poverty and just this kind of bullshit oppression. I know mine did." They nodded. "And let's face it. No one loves free enterprise and the American way more than us." That got a laugh. "We are the

American dream, my friends. I say we protect it and catch these motherfucking ISIS pieces of shit."

Gio looked around. He'd hooked them, he knew. They were all talking, stirred up. But he had to reel them in.

Gilberto, a Colombian coke lord from Elmhurst, spoke up. "I don't know, man. Us working with cops? And Feds even? That can never happen. Cats and dogs, man. And rats, too, don't forget. We got to be careful."

Gio nodded. "Tell me about it. But the fact is, it has happened before. Menachem, you remember Lucky Luciano?"

"I was just a little pisher then, but sure, I remember."

"Well, back then, during World War Two, when the government was worried about sabotage and spies on the docks, they reached out to Lucky, who was the boss at the time, because they knew he was the one who could secure the waterfront. And when the Allies were getting ready to invade Italy, he talked to his friends overseas. Mafiosi blew up Fascist installations to provide a diversion, and they tipped off our troops about where to land. Am I right?"

The Rebbe nodded. "You're a smart boy, Gio. Just like your father. And okay, like you say, we're not saints. I don't deny I have some dirt under my nails, too. But catching spies and finding bombs? Who knows how to do this? Me? You? Alonzo? Maria? We're businesspeople, like you said. And we're street people. This is a whole different thing." He wagged a finger. "And don't tell me to call the Israelis. That kind of meshugas I don't need."

Gio put his hands up. "One step at a time," he said. "All I'm saying now is what if? Hypothetically. If we did have someone. We would need to make a pact. All of us here would have to agree, and tell our other friends, to give this man free access. To grant him authority to operate across all our territories and do what he has to do to track them down."

"Like bounty hunter," Alexei said. "Or no, like the marshal in old westerns."

"Exactly!" Gio said, pointing at him.

"Whoa, whoa . . ." This was Patty White. One of the last of the old Irish mob that once controlled the West Side, still had powerful political connections, a sports book, and a crew of killers. "My dad just got locked down in a supermax thanks to a federal fucking marshal. I'll thank you to choose another word."

"Sheriff!" It was Uncle Chen. He chuckled.

Menachem patted his leg. "That's good! Sheriff. Like Clint Eastwood in the movies," he said.

Gio didn't recall Clint playing a sheriff much, but whatever, he let it go.

"All right, Gio," Alonzo said. "Let's say, hypothetically, we're in. Where in hell are we going to find us a gangster sheriff?"

Gio sat back. He could use one of those espressos about now. "Let me look into it," he said. "I've got a friend I can call."

7

Joe's guess was right. If you get invited to one, a Scottish-Korean wedding is definitely worth checking out. Luckily for everyone, the food was mainly Korean and the whiskey mainly Scottish. The music was loud, the yelling louder, and the laughing loudest. And the staff gave up trying to stop the smoking. The Korean relatives pretended not to understand and the Scottish just said, "Fook off."

Of course, as a last-minute addition, Joe was seated at a table off to the side, along with Derek; Derek's fiancée, Julie, a slim, smart Chinese girl from Forest Hills; and Crystal, from the club, who had gone all out, with a dazzling gown, updo, and sparkling makeup that looked as though it had been atomized over her light brown cheekbones and deep brown eyes. Joe was glad he had worn his one suit. Black, so that it could also work for funerals. The rest of their table were family friends: a very old Korean couple who spoke almost no English and an equally old Scottish couple who spoke with such thick accents that Joe could barely make out a word, which was even more embarrassing because in theory, they were speaking English. Then Derek whispered in his ear.

"I just got a text from Clarence, the guy I told you about. He's downstairs waiting to meet you."

Joe excused himself. Julie and Crystal moved to sit together, laughing and chatting, Crystal giving Julie hair and makeup tips for her upcoming wedding. Outside, Derek and Joe crossed the street, dodging the creeping midtown traffic, to where a man in a leather jacket leaned against a black Lexus.

"There he is." Derek nodded in his direction and the man nodded back.

Clarence looked like a project manager who had boxed a little in his youth, which is exactly what he was. Thinning hair over a thick skull, wide forehead, bent nose, expensive dental work, smooth tan. Everything he wore—the zip-up leather jacket, the polo shirt, the tan slacks, the loafers—was pricey and tasteful, and none of it fitted quite right over his broad, boxlike physique. Same for the heavy gold watch and diamond pinkie ring on his fat bruiser's paws. He was a tough guy who was smart and hard-assed enough to boss around other tough guys. Derek introduced them and he gave Joe a knuckle-crusher shake. Joe just smiled.

"Hey, Joe, thanks for coming out. Derek's good people and he vouches for you. And I asked around a bit. Folks say you're a real pro. So if you want in, the job is yours."

"What's the plan?"

"Shipment of weapons coming in tomorrow, AKs mostly, some rocket launchers, a special item or two. Some redneck is bringing them up from down south to sell illegally at a private gun show out in the woods. We hit him on the road. Us three and a friend of mine, muscle if we need it. But I doubt we will. According to my info he's just some amateur gun nut. Should be cake."

"How big is my slice?"

"I guarantee you each five grand just for the ride, even if the truck's full of pig shit. Otherwise my client has agreed to take the whole shipment at set prices per piece. Could be up to a hundred. We split four ways."

Joe thought for a minute, his gaze drifting to a cab that was inching by. The turbaned driver made eye contact and nodded, while his fares, a hipster couple, each stared into their phones. Joe nodded back.

"I'll drive," he told Clarence. "Just drive. No violence. No heavy lifting." He winked. "Bad back."

"Sure," Clarence said. "You and me will let the kids do the work." He held out a hand and Joe shook it, gently.

On the way back inside Derek was complaining. "That fiancée of mine. I made the mistake of telling her I got a job. She's already decided how to spend the dough on a dining room set for our new place. And a two-thousand-dollar couch! The couch I have now cost me a hundred bucks at Housing Works and it's fine."

Joe patted him on the back. "Might as well get used to it. Just say, 'Yes, honey' and smile."

"That's what my uncle says, too. Hey, Joe, were you ever married?"

"I can't remember."

Derek laughed. "Same old Joe. So forthcoming. Now, where are our dates anyway?"

They were on the dance floor, gyrating wildly with each other and the old Korean and Scottish couples. Jerry the giant was drunk again, bursting from his tux, but this time he was a happy drunk, dancing like a jolly beast with his tiny bride riding atop his shoulders and waving a bottle of single malt over the cheering crowd.

Meanwhile, uptown, Donna had finally gotten Larissa, her daughter, to bed after reading the same book four times—not bad, really—when the phone rang. Frantically she shut the bedroom door and then carried her purse into her bedroom and shut that door, too, then checked. It was a work call, forwarded from the office number, which she didn't do for every rando, only for the legit sources who had her direct line, though of course not her private cell. Especially not this sleazebag. Norris was a gun guy, a creep down in North Carolina, up on federal charges for selling guns to known felons, trying to earn some mercy points by informing on the other creeps. This time he had info on a shipment of stolen military hardware: AKs, rocket launchers, and other goodies. Some redneck was bringing it up north to a private gun show for sale. If the Feds planned it right, they could shut down the whole party.

Suddenly wide-awake, Donna got the details and called her contacts at ATF. She also told them she wanted to ride along as FBI liaison. Who knows? It could be her big break. In any case, it was a field trip, a ride in the country. It should be cake.

8

Joe drove. It was a windowless cargo van, painted with an innocuous U-DRIVE logo. Derek sat beside him, chattering and dialing the radio. Clarence and his muscle, an ex-con called Lex, rode up ahead in a pickup, public works green with a phony insignia, showing the way. After meeting all together to discuss the plan on Monday, Joe and Derek had spent Tuesday and Wednesday acquiring and prepping the vehicles, while Clarence and Lex saw to weapons and other gear. They left early Thursday morning, soon after daybreak, and stopped once for a piss and coffee just over the Pennsylvania state line. Only Derek was ebullient and excited. That was his nature and his way of channeling the pre-job nerves. The others were quiet, which was fine with Joe.

They drove another hour, first on a state road, then finally on a two-lane blacktop through scrubby woods and not much else worth mentioning. Finally, Clarence pulled over at an intersection. A dirt road led off to the right.

"This is me," he told Joe when he stopped the van on the shoulder behind the pickup. "You guys head down that way about a quarter mile to the blind turn and set up. You'll see the spot. Careful, though, that road's a bitch." He grinned. "It's meant to be."

"Okay," Joe said, and went back to the van. They kept watch while Clarence ducked behind the pickup and pulled on his green road worker suit, orange vest, and hard hat. Then Lex got in with Joe and Derek, taking the jump seat, still silent. As Joe turned down the dirt road, he could see Clarence in the side-view mirror, parking the pickup across both lanes.

He'd been right about this road. Rutted and narrow, it was just a country lane. Joe drove slowly, wrestling the steering wheel, avoiding the deeper ruts, and inching over the potholes. He found the spot Clarence had described. It was fine, a hard left into thick woods. He stopped, and Lex and Derek hopped out. They started unrolling the tire spikes, while Joe carefully executed a three-point turn and eased the van back among the trees. Then he put it in park, shut the engine off, and jumped out. Joe checked his watch.

"Should be about fifteen minutes," he said.

Lex got a duffel bag from the van and removed the weapons. He and Derek had assault rifles modified to fire on automatic with extra-capacity magazines. Next Lex handed out the ski masks and plastic ties before tossing the duffel back into the van. Then Lex and Derek got down in the ditches on either side of the road, positioned at an angle so as not to risk firing on each other, and Joe got back in the van, stuffing his mask and ties into his pockets.

Now when the target vehicle came around the blind turn, it would hit the spikes, blowing out its tires. Derek and Lex would come at it from both sides, ordering the driver out and hopefully tying him up without incident. At that point Joe would pull the van out, now facing back the way they'd come, and open the back doors so that Derek and Lex could easily shift the cargo from the disabled vehicle to their own. Then they'd get back in and drive out. If anyone approached from behind them, the dead truck would block the way. Clarence would be on guard at the other end, where they'd rejoin the main road. He'd abandon the pickup, which was stolen with fake plates, of course, and take the keys, thereby blocking another approach. He'd hop into the van with the others, and, if all went well, Joe would drive them away. It was a simple plan, but it was meant to be a simple heist.

9

Donna was doing sixty when she saw the public works pickup blocking the road. There were cones and a flagman waving her off. She muttered a curse under her breath. She had driven alone, intending to meet the ATF folks at their staging area, a state recreation rest stop about a mile up ahead. They planned to seal off the gun show access routes, then wait and watch till they saw the dealer with the stolen hardware arrive, grab him, and storm the show itself, looking for other illegal weapons or unlicensed sellers. It was a simple plan. But already someone had fucked it up. Roadwork should have been noted when the Feds contacted the locals. Now here was this schmo in an orange vest standing right in the path where the target was expected to come, waving a flag. She grabbed her radio.

"Base, this is Zamora. Come in."

"Go ahead, Zamora, this is Casey."

"Hi, Casey. How come no one told us about this roadwork going on?"

"Roadwork?"

"I've got a public works flagman with a detour about a mile up from you."

"We have nothing scheduled for today. Maybe there was some kind of accident? Or a tree fell? Can you tell him to clear out for an hour and come back?"

"Roger. I'll handle it." She pulled over and parked on the shoulder near the pickup, then grabbed her sunglasses before stepping out of the car. She did not grab her vest.

"Good morning," she told the broad-shouldered, unsmiling man in the orange vest and hard hat, brushing back her jacket to show the badge clipped to her belt. "FBI. What seems to be the problem here?"

Joe knew something was wrong when he heard the shots. He was sitting in the van, staring at the trees across the road. They were pines, mostly, and the air through the window smelled of pine, too, mixed with a rich undertone of mulch and rotting wood, the forest scent of both death and life. He was just noticing how still it was, how empty of man-made sound, only birds calling, a woodpecker hammering, and some kind of ambient insect hum. Then the shots came. There were three, close together, maybe from two guns. He craned his neck, peering at the road, and saw both Lex and Derek poke their masked heads above the ditches where they were lying in wait. They looked at each other, making *Who knows?* gestures with their arms. Then Lex raised a hand, signaling he had an idea, and he got out his phone. Clarence was supposed to ring when the gun dealer turned down the country lane. Lex called him. He shook his head.

"Voice mail," he yelled.

"What should we do?" Derek yelled.

"Don't know," Lex yelled back.

Joe put the van in drive. He eased out into the road, careful to avoid the spikes. He opened the door. Lex and Derek ran up, still in their masks, rifles cradled in their arms.

"Get in," Joe said.

"But Clarence said—" Lex began.

Joe cut him off. "Never mind that. Either Clarence had to change the plan or the job's off. Either way I'm not staying here."

Derek hopped in, and a beat later Lex climbed aboard. Derek climbed over to the jump seat and Lex settled in beside Joe.

"Okay," Lex said. "I just hope Clarence isn't pissed."

"Don't worry about that," Joe said as he hit the gas. "Hope he isn't dead."

10

It was the look in his eyes that first told Donna something was wrong. Panic. True, lots of folks look basically terrified when you identify yourself as FBI. Maybe they have something to feel guilty about, maybe not, but they know it's trouble. But this guy looked different, his eyes moving wildly about, as if looking for a way out of his head. Then, when he dropped his flag and stepped toward her, she instinctively stepped back. And when he reached his hand behind him, hers dropped to her gun, and she yelled, "Stop!" And when his hand came back out holding a 9mm Sig, she lifted her gun up and fired, twice, as he fired once.

His shot went wild, hitting a tree somewhere or maybe an unlucky squirrel. Her first also missed; she'd fired too quickly, before she was fully in position, and the bullet went through the side panel of his pickup. Her next round went right through the meaty part of his thigh.

He howled and went down, dropping his weapon, and she closed in, gun on him in the two-hand pose now, kicking his gun off to the side.

"Hold it right there," she ordered. "Don't move."

He nodded, hands up.

"Now roll over on your stomach," she said. "Facedown. And be smart. Next one's going through your lungs, and that's not the kind of vest that helps."

He did it. She cuffed him. Good. Donna was in control of the situation now, but what the fuck the situation was, she didn't have a clue.

She ran back to her car and got on the radio. She called for backup and let them know a suspect was shot and an ambulance was needed as well. Then she told the ATF base command that something had gone very wrong.

"What did? Who is this suspect?"

"I have no idea," Donna said. "I didn't have time to ask before he shot at me. But you better move on the gun show now. Try to seal it off. I'll stay here."

"Okay, but be careful."

"Don't worry," Donna said, a bit annoyed, as she was the only one who had done anything right so far. "I got it."

But she was wrong, about that at least, because while she was talking, another vehicle came down the highway at full speed. Seeing the roadblock ahead, the driver made a quick turn down some country road.

Joe steered the van back up the lane, going as fast as he could while still trying his best to avoid the worst pits, as Lex sat beside him, tensely holding his weapon in his lap.

"Hey, point that thing out the window," Joe told him. "It could go off if we hit a bump. And put your belt on."

"Relax, Dad. Who said you're the boss now?" he asked.

"Fine," Joe said. "You're the boss, but try not to blow any-one's balls off while you're figuring out the new plan."

"Asshole," Lex muttered, but he lowered his rifle, resting it on the window frame. It was a good thing, too, because just as they came bouncing over a big bump, the gun dealer came around the bend, going fast in his Jeep Wrangler, and ran straight into them.

Lex went through the windshield, headfirst, still holding his rifle, which sprayed bullets harmlessly into the woods as he rocketed over the hood and died. Joe, who always had his belt on, ducked and braced. He took a hard hit against the steering wheel, bruising his forearms, but he was okay. Derek got thrown from the jump seat and went rolling through the empty van, banging his shoulder and hip against the rear doors, which flew open. He was okay, too, and as soon as he got his bearings, he started searching for his gun.

The Wrangler was hardly damaged at all. Riding higher than the van, it had a broken headlight, a bent front hood, and a crumpled fender, but it would run. The driver, how-ever, was freaked. He had a load of illegal weapons, he had just seen some sort of cop or state workers blocking the road to the market where he planned to sell them, and now a body had come flying over his hood. He threw the Jeep into reverse, but no luck, his fender was hooked on the busted grille of the van.

As soon as he could focus, Joe unhooked his seat belt and hopped down. He came quickly around to the driver's side of the Wrangler, noting the crates in the back—rattled but

43

still tied down under a tarp. The goods. He also noted Lex's mangled corpse but didn't see his rifle, which had flown off somewhere, maybe into the ditch. He put a concerned look on his face and opened the driver's door.

"My God, you okay? I think my friend is dying."

"He's alive?" the driver asked, getting his belt undone.

"I think so, we need help. Please come take a look."

"Look, my fender's hooked," the driver said, climbing down. "Help me get it loose and then we can take your friend to the hospital."

"Sure," Joe said, reaching up as though to help him down, then grabbing his arm and jerking him out the door, letting the driver's own body weight slam him to the ground. He hit his knees and grunted, as Joe chopped him hard across the back of the neck. He was out.

"Derek!" Joe yelled. "Come help me get the Jeep loose!" But it turned out not to be necessary, because just then, another truck coming from the other direction, this one a four-door Ford pickup, hit the van from behind, knocking the Jeep's fender off completely and setting it free.

Derek had just found his rifle, which had bounced around the van, luckily with the safety on, and landed under a seat. He grabbed it up and jumped out the back door, just in time to see a Ford pickup with a Confederate flag front plate coming right at him.

I'm dead, he thought, and in the split second of consciousness he had left, he flashed forward to a vision of his wedding, of the traditional ceremony his fiancée's family had insisted on, which he had dreaded but now, in his vision, saw as beautiful: the procession from their family home to his, the Confucian ceremony, the elaborate banquet with shark fin soup, sea cucumber, abalone, lobster, squab. He saw his proud uncle, his crying mother wishing his father were alive. He saw his bride.

Then the truck hit the spikes. The tires blew and it spun out of control, skidding wildly. Realizing he was alive, Derek stepped aside and watched in amazement as the truck slid sideways into the back of the van. The truck was full of gun nuts, fleeing the illegal meeting that the Feds, springing from their positions in the woods as soon as Donna had sounded the alarm, had just raided. Now the gun nuts, their escape route blocked and their vehicle disabled, came spilling from the doors, wearing body armor, armed to the teeth, scared, and half drunk. They saw Derek standing there with a rifle in his arms, and thinking he was some kind of Federal cop come to revoke their inalienable rights, they shot him dead.

When the pickup sideswiped the van, ramming it against the Jeep, Joe had leaped for cover, rolling into the ditch, where he saw Lex's rifle but let it lie. He peeked over the edge and saw that the new impact had knocked the Jeep free. A moment later, he heard the bursts of automatic fire. The smart thing, now, would be to hop into the Jeep and get going, make for the open road. But where was Derek? With a sigh, he reluctantly took up the rifle, checked it quickly to be sure it was loaded and functional, and, staying low, ran along the ditch toward the shooting.

Peering out carefully, he saw Derek down on the ground, a bunch of armed men in body armor standing over him. Joe fired a burst into the air over the men, hoping to send them fleeing so that he could help Derek. Instead they turned and fired wildly, tearing the trees behind him to shreds as he took cover in the ditch. Pine needles rained down and a few cones landed softly, like eggs.

"Goddamn it," he said to himself. He crawled rapidly along the ditch and then snaked out from a spot shielded by the van, lying prone and resting his weapon on both elbows while they continued to blast the shit out of the forest. Joe took a deep breath, let it out partway, and held it. Aiming carefully, he shot one man right under the kneecap, where his shin guard and thigh protector left a gap. The man screamed as his knee was blown out and went down. Joe took a second shot, this time hitting another guy in the gap over his elbow. The guy dropped his gun and took off, cradling his shattered limb. Joe fired twice more, ripping apart the toes of a man who was wearing sneakers along with his battle gear. They fled, limping for cover behind their truck.

Joe rose up, firing bursts over the pickup as he ran to Derek, and saw in a glance that he was dead, his eyes staring up at the sky through the trees. Joe didn't hesitate; he turned and ran, firing behind him until the magazine was empty. He tossed the gun, hopped into the Jeep, started the engine, and threw it into reverse. He could see one of the gun nuts watching in confusion. He didn't even bother to shoot.

* * *

Joe reversed down the lane, going as fast as he safely could, hearing sirens and more gunfire coming from back where the van was. It was clear now that someone had called the law, but less clear was whom the law had been called on. As he got close to where the lane joined the main road, Joe spun the wheel, swinging around, and parked on the shoulder. He didn't want to risk driving out into some kind of trap. If need be, he'd ditch the Jeep and its cargo and flee through the woods on foot.

He moved quickly but carefully, dodging from tree to tree, and saw the stolen pickup where they'd left it, but now there was a black Chevy with government plates parked alongside. Getting down low, he inched forward. There was Clarence, cuffed and sitting with his back against the tire of the truck. And standing over him, peering down the highway through binoculars, was Agent Zamora, the one he'd asked to the wedding. She'd said no, of course, as he knew she would, but she had flirted, there was no denying that. And there was no way to fake that smile.

Joe pulled the ski mask over his head and came out of the woods on his belly. He crept up behind her, which wasn't that hard with her attention on the binoculars, and then, when he was within a few feet, he sprang forward and pulled her legs out from under her. She went down, binocular strap impeding her movement, and he was on her, with his knee in her back, before she could draw her gun. He used the plastic tie on her wrists, unhooked her holster, and tossed the whole thing under the car. Then he took her keys and went to Clarence. He saw that he was wounded. He leaned in close and lifted his mask up.

47

"Thank God you're here," Clarence said.

"Can you walk?" Joe asked, unlocking the cuffs.

"I doubt it."

"Okay, wait here."

"Hey, hey, where you going?" Clarence yelled, but Joe ignored him, running back to where he'd left the Jeep, a short distance now that he was running on open ground. He drove back to where the two vehicles were parked and got out. He hoisted Clarence, who moaned as he helped him into the passenger seat.

"One more thing," Clarence said. "You've got to take care of her. She saw my face, heard our voices . . ."

Joe nodded, pulling his mask back down. He took her key ring and went to the trunk of her car. Inside was the shotgun he knew she'd have and various loads. He cracked the gun, loaded it, and, while Clarence watched, walked back around to Agent Zamora. She'd managed to roll over by now and was pushed up into a half-sitting position, trying to crawl away. Joe leveled the shotgun at her. She shuddered, closing her eyes, then reopened them and stared right at him.

"Sorry," he said, and pulled the trigger.

Joe sped the first ten miles or so, gas pedal to the floor, the revolver he found in the glove box beside him, but as soon as he found the highway, he joined the traffic flow, slowing down and keeping pace with the other drivers. He tried to slow himself down, too. Before, when he'd seen the danger, his conditioning had kicked in and he felt completely calm, his mind able to function clearly, to make decisions, and his body able to react swiftly and effectively, without panic. But now the adrenaline was making him nauseated. His head ached and his skin crawled with clammy sweat. He could feel his hands trembling and gripped the wheel tighter.

But what really got him was the moaning. Clarence was delirious now, shock giving way to acute pain and confusion from loss of blood, which was slowly seeping into the seat, puddling in the leather creases. He writhed against the seat belt, and each pitiful scream when the Jeep hit even a slight bump was like a nail running through Joe's skull. Joe turned on the radio to try to drown him out, but it was some kind of religious station, a ragged voice ranting hysterically about Jesus, and that just made him feel crazier, as the noise in his own head got louder. Bugs splattered themselves on the glass before him, and the tree line blurred in a smear across the windows while the voice beseeched Jesus to save him. He punched the button. Now it was talk radio, two men arguing about something, politics or baseball, he couldn't tell. The coppery reek of fresh blood and the glandular stink of fear filled his nose. A new scream tore through him, circling his head like feedback.

"Shut the fuck up," he yelled, out loud, to everybody, and turned the radio off, but it didn't help. The scream was in his own throat now, choking him. He covered his mouth, like a hostage, and while sad whimpers leaked through the fingers, tears dripped from his eyes. All they wanted was to close.

He saw an exit for a town and took it. And at the first red light, when he was sure no one was looking, he grabbed the revolver by the barrel. Turning in his seat, he thumped

Clarence hard on the back of the head, knocking him unconscious, then gently settled him back against the seat, like a
snoozing passenger. He took a deep breath and drove on,
cruising till he saw a large chain pharmacy with a parking
lot of its own. He parked around back near the dumpsters
and got out. Then he leaned over and puked.

Part II

11

When Donna looked up and saw a masked man pointing a shotgun at her—her own shotgun, she was pretty sure—she fixed her thoughts on her daughter. She thought of her mother next and then, to her surprise, she thought of God, whom she had not considered in a couple of decades. Maybe since her father had died. But now she shut her eyes and prayed in earnest, for the welfare of her child and for her mother and for her own soul, whatever that meant, and then she thought, *Fuck this, if I'm going to die I might as well see it coming*, and she opened her eyes again. Defiant, she raised her head and looked up, from the looming barrel of the shotgun to the eyes in the holes in the mask. Somehow, to her surprise, they seemed weirdly familiar and kind. As if she almost knew who it was. She had always known death was waiting nearby, a constant companion in life and work, but she had not expected it to come as a friend, with comfort in his eyes.

"Sorry," the man said, and he pulled the trigger. The gun went off, she fell back, and there was an instant of pure . . . what? Terror? Blankness. Of thinking, *I'm dead*. Of hanging on and then letting go, like surrendering to a wave at the beach, knowing if you fight you drown, if you float you're free. And then a microsecond later: *I'm not.* She realized he had fired a beanbag round. There it was, lying beside her where it had bounced off her chest. *Holy shit, I'm alive,* she thought. *I'll hug my daughter again and kiss my mother. It's a fucking miracle*—sent by the God she didn't believe in. But still, she waited until the Jeep pulled away and she was sure they were gone before she let herself cry. And when she heard the ambulance approaching, she stopped.

After he got done puking, Joe walked around the dumpster to the back door of the drugstore. He pulled his mask back on and waited, holding the revolver at his side and spitting occasionally to try to get the awful taste out of his mouth. Finally the door opened and a young man in a pharmacist's uniform came out and lit a cigarette. Joe stepped out of the shadows and hit him on the head with the butt of the gun. Then he looked inside. He walked across a short hall into the pharmacy storage area, where a pale young woman with a lot of freckles was filling prescriptions.

"Don't scream," Joe said calmly, showing her the gun. "I won't hurt you unless you scream."

Her eyes went wide, showing white all around the green irises, but she didn't scream.

"Now you're going to stay calm and do what I say, right? I don't want to hurt you. Understand?"

She nodded.

"Okay. Here's what we're going to do. Get a bag and fill it with what I say." She jumped up and grabbed a plastic shopping bag, knocking over the pill bottle she was filling.

"Easy, easy. Stay calm. Everything's okay. Now here's what I want: rolls of gauze, surgical tape, gauze pads." She moved smoothly now, like a robot, gathering the items. "I want alcohol, a whole bottle, and dental floss and a needle."

"You mean a syringe?" she asked.

"No, I meant a sewing needle, but, yes, I will take some of those diabetic syringes, too."

She gave him a box. "I don't have a sewing needle. That's in notions."

"That's fine. Skip it. You're doing great. Just one more thing: I want Dilaudid."

Joe made the pharmacist step outside with him and then shut the door behind them so it locked. She stared in horror at her unconscious colleague.

"Don't worry, he's fine." Joe took the cuffs he'd taken off Clarence and cuffed her to the dumpster. "Sorry to have to do this," he said. "The key's right here." He placed it out of reach, near the door, and picked up the bag. "Thank you very much."

"You're welcome," she said reflexively, as he went back around the dumpster to the Jeep.

12

Clusterfuck. That, Donna believed, was the official term. And that meant the term for her current status, she supposed, was *clusterfucked.* "A little sore" was what she said when colleagues asked how she felt: Sore from the bruise where the beanbag load had struck her and left a gorgeous purple contusion. And sore from the ass-chewing her boss had provided.

But it was an ATF operation, after all, with the FBI merely providing intel, so most of the shit got on them. And even though the stolen military hardware slipped through, they did round up a bunch of black market dealers and seize plenty of other illegal arms being traded. And it was Agent Zamora who had the brains to notice something off with the public works detour. On the other hand, it was also she who let the guy escape. So . . .

In the end, she was back where she started, in the dungeon, shoveling tips. She called her source, Norris, the sleazebag gun dealer, who had just added double-crossing liar to his long list of bad character traits. He didn't pick up. The little creep was probably out selling bullets to schoolkids.

Then she sat back down at her desk, saw the pictures of her daughter and her mom, and remembered that she'd been spared. She was lucky to get away alive and with nothing really wounded but her pride. She also had a hunch, an itch of curiosity. Why hadn't that masked bandit killed her, as she heard the prisoner, the fake road worker, tell him to? And why had he apologized? He was fine with stealing weapons, assaulting officers, and helping a federal prisoner escape, but he felt bad about hurting her? What kind of villain was that?

And then there was his voice, which sounded vaguely familiar, and the funny/sad twinkle in his eyes that she swore she remembered, too. *Suspect had funny/sad eyes that I vaguely remember.* That was not in her report.

But she did go back and check the arrest logs from the other night for a name, and then typed that name into the system: Joseph Brody, a.k.a. Joe the Bouncer.

Gio's day was going fine until he got the call from Flushing. Actually he'd been on a high. Orchestrating that big meeting with all the bosses had been a real coup, in some ways the first of its kind. Sure, plenty of councils were called, but usually within one organization, like the gatherings of the Five Families in the old days, or else meetings between bosses to resolve disputes, cut deals, or end wars. But getting everyone on board, the whole town working together, was fucking historic, or so he'd been told with lots of handshakes and backslaps afterward, and he'd gone home feeling like a king. He'd taken his family out to sushi for dinner and shared his overflowing positive energy with his wife in bed that night as well. Then, after she was snoozing blissfully, he'd gone out into his backyard and smoked a cigar under the stars. And now here he was, less than twenty-four hours later, with the whole thing shot to hell.

The call came from Uncle Chen's people. Apparently Chen's nephew, a kid named Derek, had turned up full of bullets when some caper went wrong, a weapons heist out in the boondocks. The contractor who'd set it all up was MIA, a heister named Clarence, whom Gio had never heard of. Then there was someone called Lex, also a corpse, nearly headless from what Chen's sources said. And the other missing player? Joe Brody, who worked at Gio's club. Uncle Chen wanted to talk to Joe. Very badly. And very soon.

This was a problem for Gio. If Joe worked for him, then he was one of his people and Gio was responsible for him. If Gio admitted that Joe was out of pocket and, in fact, on this job without Gio's approval, then he was admitting that he could not even control his own men, much less run the kind of citywide plan he'd just talked everyone into. On the other hand, if he took responsibility for Joe's actions, then he'd be putting himself and his family in a potential conflict with Uncle Chen's people. And fucking with the Chinese Triads was something you wanted to avoid. He dialed Joe's number again. It rang and rang, and then a robot told him that the subscriber had not set up his voice mail. *For fuck's sake, why even have a phone?* He hurled his own phone at the wall so hard it shattered, and Paul, his accountant, jumped, dropping a sheaf of P&L reports. No big deal, another disposable, but still, here he was in his beautiful office behind his beautiful desk in his beautiful suit, with his beautiful,

Princeton-educated, blue-eyed WASP accountant tallying up his fortune, and he was raging and cursing and smashing phones like a street corner thug.

It showed him how much stress he was under, how close to losing control.

"Sorry, Paul," he said. "I shouldn't have done that."

"No," Paul said. "You shouldn't have." He started picking up the spilled papers.

Gio took a deep breath and then got the Scotch out and took a deep shot. He called his assistant out front and told her not to let any calls through while he was in conference. Then he said, to Paul, "Lock the door and get out the flogger." He went into the bathroom to change.

13

Joe got back on the highway and drove till he found a turnoff for a motel, a single-story U-shaped building with parking in front of the rooms and a small pool in the interior courtyard. It was near a couple of restaurants, a truck stop, a 7-Eleven, a car wash, and a three-story office building. Joe parked in back, behind some trucks. He went through Clarence's pockets and took his wallet and a Swiss army knife, then left him snoring while he went to the office, wearing sunglasses he'd found in the visor. He put a smile on his face, though his head still pounded.

"Hi there," he said to the lady behind the counter. She was chubby and white with stringy black hair and some colorfully inked roses climbing up her arms.

"Hi, can I help you?"

"I hope so. I'm beat. My cousin and I have been driving nonstop. Can we get a room with two beds? The quieter the better?"

"You're in luck," she told him, looking at her screen. "Number thirty is free. That's the farthest back."

"Terrific." He pulled out a card from Clarence's wallet, then pretended to hesitate and pulled out a hundred. "You know what, if you don't mind I'd just as soon pay cash. Been racking up the gas charges."

She laughed. "Sure, hon. I know how it is." She made change.

"And while I'm here," he added, leaning forward and grinning. "Could I maybe borrow a needle and thread? A button popped off my other pants." He laughed and she laughed with him. "And, oh yeah, scissors."

Joe stopped by the 7-Eleven, bought one beer in a bottle and some water, then pulled the Jeep around to the spot in front of the room and shook Clarence awake. He helped him inside and onto one of the beds and drew the shades. He was moaning again, so Joe opened the beer, dumped it into the sink, and used the cap and Clarence's lighter to dissolve two Dilaudids in some of the water. He unwrapped one of the syringes and filled it, pushing the liquid back up until a drop formed on the needle's tip. He took off his belt and tied Clarence's arm off, smacking his forearm till a vein swelled, then eased the painkiller in. He loosened the belt. Clarence quieted immediately, shutting his eyes. Then Joe went back out, locking the door behind him, and moved the Jeep back to its more hidden spot.

When he returned Clarence was totally out. Sliding a folded bath towel under Clarence's leg, Joe cut off the leg of his pants, exposing the wound, a jagged star torn in the thigh. He washed it with alcohol and the gauze pads, cleaning away the blood as if he was wiping a small drooling mouth. Then he used the blade of the knife to poke around gingerly until he saw the slug. He tried to draw it out with the tweezers, and managed to work it loose, but it kept slipping free, so he used the pliers to slowly extract it like a bad tooth. He washed the wound again. Then he threaded the needle with dental floss and sewed the hole shut, cross-stitching and sealing it as best as he could. Then he bandaged Clarence up.

He cleaned up, careful to put the slug, the syringe, and all the bloody gauze in the plastic bag from the drugstore. He took his own clothes off and got in the shower, turning it up as hot as he could stand it. He soaped up, washed his hair, and then stood under the showerhead a long time, letting the hot water pound his aching head and stiff shoulders. He brushed his teeth with the little free toothbrush and drank several glasses of water—getting rid of the vomit taste—but he still felt like shit. He wrapped a towel around his waist and crossed the room to peek out through the curtains. Kids were jumping into the pool, screeching, then climbing out to jump in again while their parents watched. He knew he should probably eat something, but the thought of walking back across in the sunlight, of passing people, of hearing those screeches, filled him with dread.

He pulled the curtains tight again and checked on Clarence. He was breathing steadily and his pulse was okay. Some red had seeped through the bandage, but it looked as though the bleeding had stopped. Clarence needed a real doctor soon, but he'd live. Joe got a clean syringe out and cooked up another, smaller dose of Dilaudid. This time he tied off his own arm. When he found a vein, he slid the needle in, then drew back the plunger until a tiny flower of blood unfurled in the barrel. Then, very slowly, he pressed down.

14

Cute or not, Joe Brody was a classic fuckup. Donna was a little disappointed but not particularly surprised. He might or might not be the gentleman bandit who apologized graciously before shooting her, but with his mask off, he was yet another charming loser in a long line, beginning, of course, with her own dad. Her kid's dad was the exception, the career-driven hyper-achiever and regular guy—and he'd turned out to be the biggest nightmare of all.

As for Joe, he was a hard-luck kid from Queens whose file read like a roller coaster of comebacks and blown chances. His alcoholic grifter parents died young, and he ended up with a grandmother, Gladys, who boasted an impressive, decades-long rap sheet of her own. After a host of juvenile offenses and truancies, Joe got a scholarship to St. Anthony's Academy, an exclusive local Catholic school, where he suddenly produced straight As, aced his SATs, and hit the jackpot—a scholarship to Harvard. Two years later he was expelled. This time it was for beating up frat boys, missing classes, and the final straw, scamming the other kids, though the rich parents and the school dropped the charges when he enlisted in the army.

For a while at least, it seemed he'd found a home. But sure enough, ten years later, the future bouncer was bounced again, with a less than honorable discharge. He ended up back where he started, in the old neighborhood, working at a strip club controlled, of course, by Gio Caprisi, who, as she found when she cross-referenced his file, went to the same Catholic school.

Donna was about to exit out of the file and forget it, when she noticed that his military record had not turned up on the search. Curious as to why they kicked him to the curb, she logged into the system and requested it. Locked out. Classified. High security clearance only. Donna frowned. She *was* high security clearance. She tried again, reentering her username and passcode. Another big red X and this time a warning not to proceed.

Donna sat back, absentmindedly touching the spot on her chest that still ached slightly. Why was a small-time loser who'd been booted out of the army so important that she, an FBI agent chasing terrorists for the security of her nation, wasn't even allowed to set eyes on his file? It seemed old Joe the Bouncer was interesting after all.

Gio got in the stall shower and started rinsing off. It wasn't really necessary. He could easily have washed the makeup off at the sink, stashed the blond wig and the dress back in their hiding spot, and driven home to take a shower, or even a Jacuzzi in his own luxurious marble tub. But soaping up and cleaning off helped him transition psychologically and, he supposed, scrub his conscience clean before he returned to his wife and his children. That way he left the naughty little slut Gianna behind him and went home as Gio, the family man.

Ironically, it was only when he took over the family business that this side of him had emerged, though looking back now he saw how it was always there. Of course, in the hypermasculine, weirdly sheltered world into which he was born, such things didn't even exist. He played football and baseball. He kissed girls at church dances and chased them at the pool club in the summers, and when he was fifteen his uncle took him to lose his virginity with a high-priced call girl. And though toughness was stressed, and he'd even taken some boxing lessons, the fact was that everyone knew him, so no one messed with him, and he was never bullied at all. Then one day when practice was rained out, he took the bus into a sketchier neighborhood close to his own. He had some idea about seeking out a fake ID like the one his friend had been showing off. As he was walking past a public school playground, two tough Irish kids jumped him and beat him down good, while a small crowd of kids watched, some holding basketballs or jump ropes, or licking cones. Turns out, boxing lessons aren't much help when your opponents refuse to obey the rules. The bloody nose and the black eye were no big deal, though. The big deal was his watch, which they took along with his pocket money. A gift from his grandma. If he came home without that, he would probably get beaten again, this time with his dad's belt. So, as they walked off, he went after them, pushing from behind and demanding the watch. They laughed and knocked him down again. He popped up. This went on a few times, to the amusement of the crowd. Then finally another kid stepped out.

"That's enough," he told them. "Give him his watch back."

"What?" They paused the beating and looked at him.

"I said that's enough, man. Keep the money but give him his watch back."

The bigger one, who was wearing the watch, scowled. "Fuck off, Brody. Who do you think you are? Go home, asshole. I think your grandma's calling."

Everyone laughed. This new kid, Brody, even smiled. Then before Gio could really tell what was happening, the new kid's hand came out of his pocket holding what Gio found out later was a broken piece of brick in a sock. He slammed the big kid right on the skull and he went down like a tree. Everyone went silent. Then they all fled, including the other bully. The Brody kid took the watch off the whimpering boy and handed it to Gio.

Later, when they became pals, Joe would explain that he'd been impressed with the way Gio kept getting back up and taking more hits without ever surrendering. To him that showed heart. What Gio did not dare to tell even his new best friend was that he had been strangely exhilarated, even thrilled, and that a weird joy shot through him with each punch the bigger boys had landed.

Years passed. He was running parts of the family's far-flung holdings and had gotten to know some pro dominatrices, seen leather bars, even dungeons. He was also married by then, happily, to his college sweetheart and not even tempted to cheat. But while he was having a drink with the high-level domme who ran one of the city's most exclusive dungeons, she told him something that stuck. Rather than pathetic losers, most of her clients were big winners

Marino Branch
Brainse Marino
Tel: 8336297

in the real world—they had to be to pay her rates—men of power, like CEOs, top lawyers and bankers, a retired general, even cops. These were guys who spent all day bossing people around and making decisions that changed lives: firing people, foreclosing on their homes, sending them off to prison or even to danger and death. The only way to relieve the pressure, and the guilt, was to give up control and take their just punishment.

From then on, Gio found himself fascinated with this idea. He didn't talk about it, but it was never far from his mind. He even considered telling Carol, but he was afraid of what she'd think, and honestly, he couldn't imagine her overpowering him, even just for pretend. It was always a man he pictured, a strong young man. So he found himself "checking" on the leather bars and kink joints more than he really had to. Meanwhile, as he prospered, he found a more sophisticated money guy to help him launder his profits and hide them in overseas accounts. And one night, checking the receipts at a gay S&M bar, he went to use the john, and there was Paul, his new accountant's junior partner—smart, young, and handsome—washing his hands.

15

The cave was supposed to be abandoned. That was the whole fucking point, the thing they'd been so proud of during the briefing, that made them feel clever as shit. It was an old smuggler's tunnel leading a couple of miles underground and coming up into a long-forgotten cave, hidden behind rubble and weeds now, that would put him right over the al-Qaeda compound. It hadn't been used since the old days, running opium past the Russians, and only the local warlord they were helping retake this territory remembered. Perfect.

Joe crept through the tunnel, in darkness, sometimes on hands and knees where the wooden braces had cracked, and emerged, before dawn, in the cave. With his night vision goggles, he reconnoitered the terrain, the camp, as promised, laid out below. He set up his sniper rifle and settled in to wait, maybe an hour, maybe ten, for the target, a high-level commander, to emerge. They knew which of the buildings he slept in, and they knew he'd be out sooner or later to join his men. Joe would confirm the target and take him out, then retreat back through the tunnel. He'd already wired the mouth of the cave to blow, so that when he fled, the tunnel would collapse and seal behind him.

Perhaps he was too intent on the target, who had finally emerged, laughing and chatting with a few other men. Perhaps with his earpiece in he just wasn't sharp enough to hear the approach of someone who knew this ground so much better than he did. In any case, there he was, eye pressed to the scope, waiting for permission to shoot, when he heard a scuffle off to the left and, rolling over, turned to aim his high-powered sniper's rifle at a little kid who was popping out of the cave. They both froze, looking at each other in amazement. The little boy was in raggedy brown clothes, dirt in his hair, dried snot on his nose. This was probably his tunnel, his cave, where he'd played his whole life. No doubt he knew every inch of it and had wandered in from another underground branching. Joe smiled and tried to speak a few words of Pashto, telling him, "Don't worry, you're safe." But apparently the kid didn't believe him or didn't understand, and meanwhile, right at that moment, the voice in his ear said, "Take him, Falcon, target confirmed. Are you there, Falcon? Come in. Take your target," and that distracted him for a split second. Maybe he even moved a fraction of an inch. Whatever it was, the kid spooked, like a stray cat, and took off at full speed, running back into the cave. He knew it well, but of course he didn't know the trip wire Joe had hooked up, and as Joe screamed, *"Stop,"* the kid screamed, too, while the cave exploded all around him, blowing him to pieces as the rubble fell.

*   *   *

Joe woke up the way he always did, with a jerk, right when he heard that scream and that explosion. Breathing hard, he looked around him, trying to guess where he was. On his cot in his tent? Or back at the base? Or in a dusty back room down a dark alley? They said he was heroic because, after the cave blew, he'd re-aimed his rifle; found his target, who was now ordering his men up to investigate the cave; and taken him out with a single bullet between the eyes, before fleeing over open ground—the cave now impassable—pursued by the enemy and holding out till the chopper came in to extract him. He didn't feel heroic. He'd merely completed the mission, no matter what, as he'd been trained, and then survived as he'd always done. Later, when he was with the old warlord's youngest son and saw his stoned eyes, he'd gone off with him to a dark, dusty room and smoked up some of the opium that his family made so much money smuggling.

"Hey," a voice said. "Wake up."

Joe rubbed his eyes. His vision cleared. He was in a motel room. He remembered.

"Hey, it's time to go. Here's coffee."

Joe sat up. Clarence was sitting on his own bed across from him, smiling. Joe could see that he'd changed his own bandage and made two Styrofoam cups of coffee from the instant the hotel had provided. Joe took it and drank.

"I guess you're alive," he said to Clarence.

"Yeah." He smiled. "Thanks to you. I owe you. Big-time."

Joe got up and started dressing. "Now what?"

"Now we go. I called my people. They're waiting for us at the safe house where we turn over the goods, with a doctor, clean clothes, food, everything we need."

Joe zipped his jeans up. He drew his belt through the loops. "All I need is my money."

16

It was six A.M. Donna had finished her morning yoga routine and was just settling down to meditate before she woke Larissa, or, as sometimes happened, she fell back to sleep and Larissa woke her, when the CIA knocked on her door. At least they knocked. She was in her underwear and a T-shirt, so she pulled on sweats, thinking maybe it was the super, since her mom, who had the key, wouldn't bother to knock. If Donna ever again had a man stay over, she'd have to remember to put the chain on.

She peeked through the peephole and there he was, suit and tie, sharp haircut, fresh shave, at six A.M.: her friendly local CIA field agent, Mike Powell. With a sigh and an unconscious hand smoothing her hair, she unlocked and opened the door.

"Keep your voice down," she said.

He smiled. "Good morning to you, too," he whispered.

"What do you want?"

"I'll start with coffee if you don't mind." Still smiling.

"If you wanted coffee you should have stopped at the place downstairs. And if you wanted me to say good morning you should have brought me one. Now what do you want?"

"Fair enough." He dropped the smile. "Why are you investigating Joe Brody?"

Donna stepped back from the door. "Come in. I'll make coffee."

She crossed to the sink, started filling the pot. He shut the door gently behind him, then took a seat at the kitchen table while she spooned in the coffee and set it to brew. She got two cups out and the milk and sugar, giving herself time to gather her thoughts, as he, being a trained CIA interrogator and general sneak, could probably tell.

"Still take milk and sugar?" she asked.

"Please."

She poured milk into both cups, then spooned sugar just into his. The coffee was brewing now, steaming and sighing and smelling good, but it would take a few minutes more, so she turned around and leaned against the counter.

"So what did you want to know?"

"Joe Brody," he repeated. "What do you know about him?"

She shrugged. "Nothing. He's a bouncer in a titty bar."

"What else?"

"Well, my sources indicate that they give hand jobs in the back room. Why? Have you finally been transferred to the jerk-off unit where you belong?"

He laughed, and she had to grin, too. Then she turned to pour the coffee, and he took off his jacket and leaned back. She put the mugs on the table and sat. They both took a sip.

"It was nothing," she told him. "A routine follow-up after a sweep. He works at a club with OC ties but seems—or seemed—like a nobody till his file turned out to be booby-trapped. So now you tell me. What's so special? Why does the CIA care?"

At first, most of what Powell told her was just what she knew: the rough childhood, the early promise, Harvard, more drama, expulsion, the military. But what she didn't know was that in the army he again showed some talent, of a more particular kind, and was quickly tapped for Special Forces training. Over the next decade he carried out classified missions all over the world. Then it seems trouble caught up to him again. He got a little too fond of those high-quality Afghani opiates and was quietly dumped back in the States.

"So what were the missions?" Donna asked.

Powell shrugged. "I don't know."

Donna rolled her eyes. "Please. If you wanted to play secret agent, you didn't have to drive up here at six in the morning."

He laughed again. "No. I mean I really don't know. Because when I opened his top secret file, there was nothing in there. All of Joe Brody's missions have been deleted. As far as we're concerned, they never happened."

"Oh."

"Yeah. Exactly. That's not a good sign." He finished his coffee. "So you were right in the first place. He is a nobody, but he's a nobody of interest. Which is why I drove up here at six in the morning, to see what Joe Nobody is up to these days. It could be big trouble if he were to join up with the bad guys."

"Which bad guys exactly?" Donna wondered aloud, but before Powell could answer, Larissa walked in, rubbing her eyes, looking angelic, too-long hair in a crazy cloud, barefoot under her nightgown.

"Daddy!" she shouted in glee, and ran over to jump into his lap. "Did you come to drive me to school?"

"That's right, princess," he said, giving her a squeeze and a kiss. "That's exactly why I'm here. Now why don't I help you get ready while Mommy gets dressed for work?"

17

It was while they were driving to the safe house that Clarence started on Joe about the next job.

"I'm just saying," he said. "You're going to be there anyway. You might as well listen."

Joe was driving. Clarence had given himself another shot of Dilaudid, less than what Joe had given him, but still he was feeling no pain. They'd swapped out the license plates with another car in the lot before they left, in case the cops had a BOLO on their vehicle by now. Better to swap vehicles, but it wasn't practical with the back full of gear and one man wounded. Plus, their destination was close and their route all secondary roads. Initially, the plan had been to steal the weapons, drive their own truck here to unload, then disperse and head back to the city in a less conspicuous fashion. But the plan had changed, and now Clarence was talking about changing it again.

"Look," Clarence said. "I didn't mention it before because I'm using a different crew, but this heist was just to get the gear we need for a bigger job—much bigger."

"Why not the same people?"

"Security. To keep everything disconnected and everyone on a need-to-know basis."

"Then I guess I don't need to know."

"That's what I'm saying. You proved yourself. Shit, you saved my ass. And we need one more man for this, so I'm saying, if you want in, you're in. When we get there, check out the plan."

"No offense, but this last plan didn't really turn out so well."

Clarence shrugged. "Shit happens. And I know what went wrong yesterday."

"You've got a rat in your house."

"Yeah. A little redneck rat. The same two-bit shitkicker that tipped us off about the shipment in the first place." Clarence smiled. "But don't worry. I told my people about that, too. He won't be kicking any more shit. There it is." He pointed. "Make that turn down this little road. It's on the right."

It was an ordinary two-story house, yellow siding and a screened porch, set far back on a good-sized piece of land. Overgrown yard, apple trees, and a big, decrepit barn with open doors that Joe pulled right into. Already inside were a black van and a late-model Volvo sedan.

Joe parked. He took off his seat belt, grabbed his jacket, and when he felt the phone zipped in the pocket he remembered that he hadn't checked it since he turned it off before the job. He switched it on. It buzzed angrily and showed a bunch of missed calls and texts, all from Gio, who had given him the phone when he started at the club and was one of only a couple of people who had the number.

"Anyway," Clarence was saying, "before we go inside and meet the others, I just wanted to say it's your choice. You can have twenty grand now, your cut, and walk away, or you can join up for this next job and have ten times that."

Joe glanced over Gio's texts:

Your friend from Flushing's family are very upset. Had to cancel wedding.

They are all looking for you now.

Uncle C is pissed. Don't go home.

And so on. Joe turned the phone back off. He turned to Clarence. "You're right. It doesn't hurt to listen."

18

Mike Powell loved his daughter. Donna had to admit that. He was a decent enough dad: Paid his child support. Showed up for his weekends. Took an interest in Larissa's drawings and dance class. Never lost his temper or raised his voice. Or that's what you thought at first, until you got to know him.

Because that was his MO all over. The clean-cut straight arrow. The right guy who showed up on time, got the job done, had maybe one beer he didn't even finish; the designated driver at the party with good credit, who broke up the fights. What a relief he'd been after her usual suspects, the drinkers and gamblers and players like her dad, who disappeared and reappeared throughout her childhood and then died drunk driving when she was nine. With them it was all fun and games, romance and adventure at the beginning, then high drama and bad comedy at the end. Mike was different, she thought. And she was right. He was. She just didn't understand how.

It started with the jealousy. Whom she talked to, what she wore, why she laughed at so-and-so's jokes at dinner—her cousin's husband, for Christ's sake, gross—or what her male coworker wanted when he called late at night. (Duh. She was an FBI agent, and so was he. He wanted her to investigate a federal crime.) Then came the control, or the attempt to, since she wasn't about to be broken. He wanted to handle the checking account and put her on an allowance, from her own paycheck. He wanted to schedule her time, decide when they should exercise, eat, even fuck, not that that went on much after she got pregnant. He never hit her, but the rage when he lost his temper, the yelling and shouting, made her think that he could, or maybe would, except that he knew deep down she would shoot him if he tried. And she was a better shot than he was, which he hated.

The final straw was when she found out he was spying on her. Checking her phone. Following up on her work schedule, using his CIA clearance or contacts to make sure she really was where she said. Actually following her, tailing her like a suspect, except she was a trained agent herself and she caught his ass, sitting in a car outside the brunch place her girlfriend had taken her to.

He fought dirty during the divorce, too, hinting that she'd had an affair, trying to take custody of Larissa, but when the judge ruled and the papers were signed, he fell in line. That was him, too. In the end he respected authority. He followed orders. He would have made a great Nazi, she thought, as she got to her desk, turned on her computer and, mentally consulting the next name on her shit list, picked up the phone and tried again to reach her treacherous dirtbag of an informer, Norris.

19

Joe listened. After they parked the car, Clarence had led him into the main house through the kitchen door, where they saw a middle-aged Indian man in a tracksuit sitting at a round wooden table and a young black kid making pancakes at the stove. The Indian man turned out to be Dr. Virk, who immediately took Clarence upstairs. The kid was on the job.

"I'm Juno," he said. "You hungry?"

"I'm Joe. And yes, I'm starved."

Juno nodded and dished out pancakes, bacon, fried eggs. He poured coffee and set a container of OJ out. Then he called in the others while Joe sat down and started to eat. Two more came in, a man and a woman, both white and probably in their late twenties. The man, Don, was British, with sandy hair and a red face, and from his demeanor—the way he spoke and the weight lifter physique—Joe made him right away for a mercenary. The woman was Yelena, with a Russian accent, white-blond hair, and dark eyes. She was quiet, lithe, and watchful, and Joe wasn't sure what to make of her. Juno was a teenager from Bed-Stuy, which Joe understood fine.

Breakfast conversation was minimal, mostly "Please pass this" and "Do you want more of that," and they were all too professional to talk about the job until it was time to. Joe and Juno went back and forth a little about places they both knew. Who made great pancakes. Which club had a badass sound system. Yelena lit a cigarette. Juno coughed and made a face. She rolled her eyes and muttered, "Americans," and went outside.

Joe was doing the dishes, Juno was helping, and Don wasn't, when Clarence came back and called them all into the living room, which was furnished in a homey style. He was wearing loose-fitting sweatpants now and a zip-up hoodie, and walking with a cane, but he seemed fine, holding a rolled-up sheet of paper in his other hand. "Thanks, Doc," he said as Dr. Virk left, and then sat down in a wing chair. Juno and Yelena sat on the couch; Juno was slouched back with his feet on the coffee table; Yelena was relaxed but on the edge of her seat, spine straight, as though ready to leap up, into either a ballet or a fight. Joe and Don took wooden chairs across from each other, as though instinctively on opposing sides.

"Okay," Clarence said, "here's the deal." He rolled the paper out across the coffee table. It was a map, fairly detailed, showing a building and the surrounding grounds. "This is the location. It's in Westchester. Basically there are three levels of security we need to get by. First, an outer fence and gate, with security guards, cameras, plus a constant field of radio waves alerting them to any motion on the grounds."

"What's that mean?" Don asked.

"It's like a small-scale radar setup. They have transmitters signaling each other all over the joint. If you break the wave, you show up on the screen."

"What about the building?" Yelena asked.

"The building itself is the easy part, or anyway the simple part. Windows sealed and alarmed. A front door with guards and elevators. A service door on the side. Nothing that would give you any trouble." She smiled just slightly as he went on. "But the next part is trickier. The room we are trying to break into. It's on the fifth floor but it has no windows. One entrance, magnetically controlled. Access restricted to handprints and iris checks."

Juno whistled, impressed. "No other door?"

"Not really. There's an alarmed fire exit to the roof, but that is solid steel, and if it opens it not only calls the cops, it autolocks everything, even disables the iris and print access and seals that door. That way the whole thing's fireproof, too. And that's hardwired direct, so no way to cut it from outside."

"That's pretty slick, I must say," Juno told him.

"It sure is. And part three is the walk-in vault. State of the art, temperature controlled." He turned to Yelena. "That's why you're here." Now she smiled for real. "I have specs to show you later."

"With all this security, what the hell are we stealing?" Don asked. "Diamonds? Gold?"

Yelena said, "Climate-controlled vault. It must be art. Paintings or antiques."

Clarence shook his head and grinned. "Nope. Even better," he said. "Perfume."

"Fuck off," Don said.

"Damn," Juno said. "I knew that stuff was pricey, but . . ."

Clarence explained: "Turns out there is this shit that sperm whales puke up."

"What?" Juno said. "Puke? Sperm? Shit? I can take you to some subway stations you want to smell that. For free with my MetroCard."

"Fuck off," Don blurted. "Now I know you're taking the piss."

"Ambergris," Yelena said.

"Who?" Juno asked.

"Ambergris is the thing you are speaking of."

"On the nose," Clarence said. "It's worth a ton. They use it in perfume and other things, too. Like ylang-ylang, some kind of thing from Madagascar. Anyway, some of this stuff is worth a fortune, like thousands of dollars an ounce."

"Fuck me," Don said.

"So we're stealing, what, like a barrel of it or something?" Juno asked.

"No," Clarence said. "We're stealing the sample, like the prototype for the new batch. Then some other lab somewhere can copy it and beat them to the market. They'd make millions."

"So it's like getting a disc of the new *Star Wars* movie or something," Juno said.

"Right. Except not a copy. We steal the movie."

"All right, I'm down," he said. "I mean, what the fuck, selling perfume's got to be easier than selling dope."

"It sounds completely cracked," Don said. "But I'm in."

"We sell this one vial for a million dollars," Clarence said, "split it five ways. Yelena, you in?"

"Yes, of course," she said. "I didn't come here just for breakfast."

"Joe?" Clarence asked.

Joe shrugged. "Let's hear the plan."

"Okay," Clarence said, leaning on the cane to stand. He grunted softly. "Let's go look at the toys."

In the barn they started unloading the Jeep. Don opened one crate with a crowbar and pulled out an AK-47. "Good," he said, and handed it to Yelena, who checked it expertly. Next he found a grenade launcher. "Better," he added. Then he opened a large crate and frowned. "Think this is for you, mate," he said to Juno.

"Oh yeah, baby," Juno said, lifting out what looked like a toy plane or a *Star Wars* collectible. "This is all for me."

"Drone?" Joe asked him.

"Yup, but this is like the Jedi starfighter of drones."

"And that's good."

"Hell yeah. You've heard about stealth fighter jets?"

"Some."

"Okay, so this baby is like a stealth drone. I can send it in right over the fence and it won't show up on their radar. Then I can use the onboard technology to jam it so they don't see you all, either. I can hack into their system, too, fuck with the alarm, the cameras, even open the door so you can walk right in like you're home for Christmas dinner."

"Nice," Joe said.

"Yes, this is good, Juno," Yelena said. "And I can crack the safe. But what about the hand and iris printing? Who has access?"

"Three people," Clarence said. "One, the CEO. I forget his name but it doesn't matter, because he's at a conference in Tokyo and then traveling in Asia all next week. Two, the designer. They call her the 'Nose,' and she has a very long Italian name that I know but can't pronounce. But that doesn't matter, either, because she's traveling with the CEO."

"And three?" Don asked.

"The chief chemist. His name I know, Bob Shatz, and he's our man. He's there like clockwork, five days a week."

"No worries," Don said. "I got two ways to solve that. One . . ." He racked his rifle. "I put this to his head and he opens the fucking door."

"Except," Clarence said, "there's a guard standing right by him as he does it, and one at a desk outside the door at all times. There're guards, people everywhere. And he has assistants who are waiting there every morning for him to let them in. Nope." He shook his head. "Too messy. We have to go in at night."

"Okay then, option two," Don said, and this time he drew a knife, a big bowie he had in a sheath under his arm. "We cut off his hands, pop out his eye, and we're in."

"That's pretty cold," Juno said.

He shrugged. "Sorry if that rattles you, but there you go."

"Also messy," Yelena said with a shrug.

"Hell yeah," Juno added. "Dude's going to have hooks and an eye patch. Be like a Halloween pirate for life."

"You have background information on this Shatz?" Yelena asked. "Maybe we get to him some other way."

"Oh yeah," Clarence said. "I sat on old Bob for a week, and what a week it was. Monday he goes to work, brings his lunch, after work goes home alone and watches TV. Tuesday, goes to work, brings lunch, goes home to watch TV. Weds, same thing, work, lunch, but get this: after work he goes bowling. Then Thursday he's had too much excitement, so after work he just goes home to watch TV."

"Okay, we get it. He's a boring fucking wanker," Don said.

"And the weekend?" Yelena asked.

"You didn't let me finish. Friday night is party night. After work he stops by a strip club, has one beer and a few lap dances, then goes home and orders pizza. Saturday—"

"Wait," Joe said. Everyone looked at him. It was the first time he'd really spoken up. "Where is the strip club?"

"The Bronx. Someplace called Circus City."

"I know it," Joe said. "Did you see what kind of girls he likes?"

"Redheads. Definitely. He dropped, like, a hundred on one."

He turned to Yelena. "If you're willing, I've got an idea that might work. No mess at all."

"I like the sound of that," Clarence said.

"Me, too," Juno muttered as he fiddled with the drone.

"Let me see if it works," Joe said to Don. "If not, you can always chop him up."

Don frowned but said nothing, testing the edge of his knife.

"What must I be willing for?" Yelena asked him.

Joe looked at her. "To wear a wig. And maybe to get naked."

She laughed. "Don't worry about it. Wigs I have plenty. And I can kill a man just as easy naked or not."

Joe smiled. "In that case," he told Clarence. "I guess I'm in."

20

Yesterday, when Agent Zamora called, Norris had been with a client. He was out in the backyard, watching while the client, a scrawny white guy with a ponytail and bushy beard, fired a TEC-9 at a bunch of bottles. The gun was obviously stolen, with a filed-off serial number, but the client didn't mind, since he was a criminal planning to use it for a bank robbery. Norris wasn't sure how that was going to go, since the client was a terrible shot and kept moving closer to the bottles, wasting ammo. Not that Norris cared—he'd already have his money—but with all the racket, he didn't hear his phone ring. Later he saw that she'd left a message, telling him to call back, but by then he was drinking beer with the client and another buddy who had turned up, and he sure wasn't calling her in front of them. Agent Zamora was his FBI handler, whom he'd never met but who sounded hot, though sort of ethnic. What kind of name was Zamora? Anyway, Norris had made a deal with the Feds to feed them information in return for making his own charges for illegal sales go away. That was his business, getting people weapons, and when he couldn't supply them directly he sometimes, for a price, helped people find someone who could. A middleman, like. So when this guy Clarence showed up with a whole lot of cash wanting a special order, something strictly military, Norris had checked into it. Turned out someone had recently stolen that very piece of property, but some other dealer, one of Norris's competitors, had already found a buyer for it up north. So Norris sold Clarence the tip on the sale and killed two birds with one stone: hopefully the second dead bird would be Jed, that asshole rival dealer, and Clarence was the stone. Then Little Miss Zamora had called. She was looking for intel about the stolen military equipment and also reminded him that he was looking at prison if he didn't come up with something good soon. So he'd given her the same tip, which was all he had to give at the time, figuring the Feds would swoop in, arrest or shoot everybody, and he'd end up killing who knows how many birds with, like, two or three stones, depending on how you counted.

Anyhow, with one thing and another—going with his client and his other buddy to shoot pool and have some more beers, then for burgers, then back home to down a few more and pass out in front of the TV—he never got around to calling her back. He'd had enough of her shit to last a while. And in the morning, he was busy in his work-shop, the garage, working on a special order, modifying a shotgun. He locked the gun in the vise and then, with his handheld metal-cutting saw, he chopped the barrel. He got out his welding torch and was all set to add the laser scope when the phone rang. Her again. He picked it up, feeling sly. "Hey there, special agent, you calling to say thanks?"

But she was not calling to say thanks. In fact she was pissed, yelling at him, accusing him of tipping off a heist crew about the dealer along with her, calling him a sleazeball scumbag and lots of other shit that he did not intend to take from any woman, especially not a brownskin. Then she mentioned that Clarence had gotten away with the weapons, and Norris was too busy being terrified to be righteously angry. He told her he needed protection right away in exchange for his cooperation. She laughed and told him to screw off, that this info had earned him zero points. In fact, he owed *her*, and he should call back when he had something of value to trade. Then she hung up.

Norris stood with the phone in his hand, thinking. He could use a beer, was his first thought. Then he figured he'd take the cash he had hidden in the house and lie low somewhere, down in Florida, maybe, do some fishing and figure this out, come up with something to put him back in good with the Feds and then go into witness protection, maybe get a name change or something. Or even better, just wait it out till they caught Clarence. He was the fugitive, after all, not Norris. He was the one being hunted.

That thought calmed him, so he wasn't that rattled when the couple walked into the workshop. It was a tall, thin dude with blue eyes and dark hair, and a blond girl who looked like a cheerleader, sexy and full of pep.

"Good morning!" she called out. "Are you Norris?"

"Yeah," he said, wondering how she knew that. "But we're closed now. I'm heading out. Sorry."

"Nothing wrong I hope?" the dude said. "Like a family emergency?"

"No. Well, yeah, actually, my mom's sick."

"Aw, that's too bad," he said, picking up the handsaw and flicking the power switch on.

"Hey! Put that down!" Norris said, but before he could take a step, the cheerleader kicked him right in the nut sack. Hard. He gasped, fighting both to breathe and not to puke as he bent double, grabbing his groin.

"Don't worry," she said, reaching for the blowtorch, firing it up. "We'll give your toys back. As soon as you tell us what you told the FBI about Clarence."

Norris went for the gun, the .45 he kept under his workbench, but even as he was reaching his arm out for it, the blue-eyed dude was bringing down the saw.

21

After transferring all the stolen equipment to the van, they stripped the Jeep of plates and other evidence and left it in the barn. The couple Clarence had rented the house from would dispose of it once things cooled down. Then Clarence and Don drove the van to a nondescript business hotel in Yonkers, just north of the Westchester county line. Joe, Yelena, and Juno took the Volvo into the city to get whatever supplies they needed. The others all had overnight bags with them, so they stopped on the way at a Walgreens, where Joe bought a pack of socks, a pack of boxers, and a pack of black T-shirts.

"What?" he said as he tossed the stuff into the back and got in. Yelena and Juno were both grinning.

"Nothing," Juno said as they pulled away. "You do travel light, though, bro."

"I didn't realize we were going on a honeymoon."

"Still. No toothbrush?"

"Or shampoo or razor?" Yelena asked from the back.

"I figure the hotel will have all that."

"I think maybe your mom buys you these underwear packs, no?" she asked with a smile in the rearview. Juno laughed. Joe laughed, too. "Close," he said. "My grandma."

When they got to the city, Juno directed Joe to a high-end electronics store downtown near Wall Street. He hopped out with a pocketful of cash from Clarence.

"Give me about an hour," he said. "Got to geek out with the nerds a bit."

"Right," Joe said, "pick you back up here," then drove a few more blocks to the shop Yelena needed. It was lower-end but just as specialized, catering to performers, with a wide array of wigs, theatrical makeup, and lingerie, the more spangled and sequined the better. "I'll find parking and meet you inside," he told her.

"Don't bother," she said. "I don't need help from a man who buys his underwear in a bag. Just meet me back where you get Juno." She opened the door. "And don't worry. I promise you will be pleased with what I choose."

She shut the door, and Joe watched her enter the store while he waited for the light to change, then he crawled a couple of blocks more and parked illegally. As long as it was not a tow-away zone, he didn't care about tickets. In a couple of days this car would be ditched, and the names on the paperwork were all fake anyway. He bought a pack of gum at a deli to get some change and then wandered a few blocks till he found a rare working pay phone, asking the operator for the FBI's New York headquarters. When the switchboard answered he asked for Agent Donna Zamora. They put him through and it went to voice mail. He hung up and checked his watch: 1:30. She could be on her lunch break or in a meeting. Or she could be in a hospital, with internal injuries from a beanbag load fired too close. Realizing he was just a few blocks from the federal building, and that he had time to kill, he started walking, not entirely sure why he was doing this or what he had in mind to do when he got there.

Along the way, he bought a Yankees cap and put on the sunglasses he'd taken from the Jeep, and when he arrived out front at Foley Square, he bought a hot dog and a water from a cart, then found a bench under a tree with a view of the employee entrance. He sat and ate, watching people come and go: finance guys in white shirts, bright ties, and suspenders, and women in sharp, severe suits. Tourists looking for Ground Zero. Government workers in more sedate suits. Harried-looking civilians with papers under their arms, looking to get something stamped, or filed, or fixed. Forty minutes passed and he was thinking he'd need to give up soon. Then he saw her. Agent Zamora came around the corner in a different suit, this time navy, and a pale gray blouse, walking and talking with a young black guy in a well-cut navy suit of his own, white shirt, red tie, tightly buzzed hair. Another agent, no doubt. They hugged—nothing romantic in it, Joe noted, and spotted a wedding ring on the guy's finger as well. Then the agent headed inside while she got in line at the coffee cart. Joe got up and stood behind her.

He was perfectly within his rights to do so. He was not under suspicion for anything, yet, and no one was looking for him, so far. He was unarmed. He could have walked right into the building and asked to use the men's room if he wanted. But he also realized that this was unnecessary, a needless complication, and just the sort of irrelevant trouble a professional would avoid. Only necessary trouble was worth the time and risk. Then again, life itself was a necessary trouble, sex a complication. And there was no love without risk. Some games have no pros.

Agent Zamora was next in line now, and with a few people waiting behind him, Joe was right up close to her, close enough to smell her glimmering hair if he wanted to, or kiss her neck, or whisper in her ear. It was strange to think that their only contact, the only touch between them, had been her nails on the bracelets as she cuffed him behind his back, or the bruise his shot must have left, like a purple-and-black flower on her skin.

Agent Zamora stepped up to the window of the cart, where a young Yemeni man was making coffees.

"Hey, secret agent!" he said. "How's it going? Ready for a latte?"

"Hi, Sameer," she said with a smile. "I am so ready."

The young man got to work, expertly pulling an espresso and steaming milk. "Catch a bad guy today?" he asked her. "Cinnamon?"

"I'm trying," she said. "Yes, please."

"Keep trying," he said, handing her the coffee. "I know you're going to get him."

"Thanks," she said, "I will," and turned to go.

Sameer yelled, "Next," at Joe, but Joe was already gone, walking quickly the other way, into the crowd, unwrapping a piece of gum. He didn't look back, but if he had, he would have seen Agent Zamora peering curiously after him, before turning to go inside. Back at the car, he found a ticket on the windshield and tossed it, along with his Yankees cap, into the trash.

Donna, meanwhile, was getting back to her office a bit late from lunch. Still thinking about Joe and if that had really been him, she was already feeling a little out of balance. And the first message she checked knocked her completely off center, so that she sat her butt right down in her chair.

Norris the creep. Her shitkicker informer had been found dead, in his own gun workshop. And it looked as though he'd been severely, and sadistically, tortured.

22

Uncle Chen was being reasonable, patient, even generous. After all, he was known as a reasonable, patient, generous man, or at least one whom everyone was too scared to disagree with. In this case he waited a full twenty-four hours before he moved on Gio. Really, this was indulgent, since the trip to Flushing from Gio's club or whatever hole in Jackson Heights this Joe character slept in would be, like, thirty minutes, forty-five with traffic. He liked Gio; he'd known him his whole life, and his father before him.

But when a day passed after his nephew's death, and Gio still told him that he could not reach his man and had no idea where he was, but that he was certain he had no involvement in Derek's killing, Uncle Chen began to lose patience. And he sent Gio a little message, a reminder that even his patience had a limit.

Gio, meanwhile, was waiting for his daughter to get her shit together so he could drive her to soccer practice, calculating how late they were and trying not to lose his own patience, when his wife pulled him into the kitchen and started whispering.

"Nora wants to talk to you about something."

"Okay." He checked his watch. They had fifteen minutes. "It better be something short, because we're late."

"She got her first period this week."

"Jesus," he blurted loudly. "Is she all right?"

"Shhh . . . of course she is. And keep your voice down."

"Sorry," he whispered. "You just caught me off guard. Give me some fucking warning next time."

"What do you mean? What next time? Having a daughter is the warning. It's not like we didn't know this was coming. It's a good thing. She's growing into a young woman as her body blossoms."

"I know, I know. I'm just, you know, wrapping my head around it."

"Well, wrap it up quick." She crossed her arms, gave him her therapist look. "Because you cannot shame her or make her feel bad about her body's natural processes. You'll give her a complex. The father's support is key."

"Yes. I realize that. Thank you. But." He put his hand on her shoulder and lowered his voice again. "Why talk to me? Isn't this the mom's department?"

"We did, and when we got on the topic of sex—"

"Sex? Jesus, Carol, you trying to tell me—"

"Not like having sex specifically. Calm down. That's not even in the picture. Here. You're sweating." She handed him a napkin. "I was just, you know, opening up a dialogue about how her life was going to start changing now." She frowned.

"Anyway, she asked if I was going to tell you and I said yes, of course, and then she said she had some things she wanted to discuss . . . privately with you."

"Oh, I see . . ." He could tell that this bugged the shit out of Carol, which made him feel a little better, while also making him very uneasy about what the hell it could be. "Well, you know how moody teens are."

"Dad!" Nora's voice came booming as she galloped down the stairs. Gio jumped like he'd just been caught at something. "Dad, let's go. We'll be late!"

"Okay, honey, coming!" he yelled.

"Anyway," Carol whispered at him. "She wants you, so get your shit together, Gio, and you know, man up."

"So," Gio said to his daughter, who was strapped into the seat beside him staring down into her phone. He searched his mind for a conversation opener. "How's things?"

She looked up at him. "Did Mom tell you about my period yet?"

He flinched a little but played it off pretty well, he thought, by looking at the road and signaling, then glancing left over his shoulder and changing lanes. "Yes, she did, honey. That's great. I mean . . . natural." He glanced at her, saw her big brown eyes on him, then stared straight ahead and cleared his throat. "Look, to be honest, I kind of always assumed you'd want to talk to your mom about these things. I mean, she's a woman and a shrink, therapist, whatever. I'm just"—he waved his hand—"you know."

"I know, Dad. But that's kind of why. I mean, I told Mom first because I needed her to get me tampons and stuff and I knew you couldn't deal with that."

He shrugged. Fair enough.

"And also because, oh my God, I know it would, like, kill her if I didn't."

He chuckled.

"But it's like she's almost *too* into it, you know? Like I totally understand why they say shrinks' kids are the most fucked up."

"What? Who says that? You think you're fucked—I mean messed up?"

"No, God, calm down. Watch where you're going. You're going to hit that car. I mean that's my point. Mom and I are super close and everything, but I feel like I need healthy boundaries with her. I don't know, in some ways I feel you and me are more alike."

"Oh yeah?" Gio smiled. "How?"

"You know, not so into feelings."

"What? What do you mean? You know you and your brother mean more to me—"

"Yes, yes, Dad. I know you love us. That's not what I mean. I just—You're more, like, I don't know, reserved. Private about things. And I can respect that."

"Thanks."

"That's why as soon as the sex talk came up with Mom, she was all over me with books and videos, and I'm, like, afraid to even say anything, but I feel like I can talk to you and you will keep it just between us." She eyed him carefully. "And not be weird."

"Of course, honey."

"Okay." She took a deep breath. "So remember last week when my team had that victory party after we beat the Wildcats?"

"Yes," he said calmly, but thought, *Holy shit, was she roofied? Attacked? If anyone gave or even offered her drugs, I will skin him alive.*

"Well, there was some kissing."

"You mean . . ."

"Just. Kissing. Okay? That's all. First base."

"Oh." Gio felt his blood pressure ease. "Okay. Well, that's fine baby. It's a natural process of blossoming into, you know . . ."

"Dad. Think about it. The party? My soccer team? It's all girls?"

"Oh."

"I mean, it was no big deal. We were all doing it, just joking around and just this once. But . . . I feel kind of weird about it now."

"Don't feel bad . . ."

"I don't." She looked at him, then down. "I kind of liked it."

"Oh."

"I mean, I only ever kissed one boy so far, Ethan Steinberg, playing spin the bottle at Lillian's bat mitzvah, and I guess I liked that, too. I just—I'm asking . . . what if I turn out to be gay? What would you think?"

Gio pulled into the lot. They could see some of her teammates on the field warming up, ponytails whipping as they bounced white balls from foot to knee to foot, or stretching

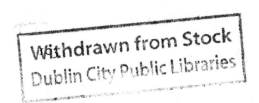

on the newly cut glass-green grass. Others were getting out of cars, huge bags slung on narrow shoulders with their names written across them. He stopped, put the car in park with the engine running. He turned to her, smiling, and took her hand. "Honey," he said. His phone buzzed in the console between them. A text. *Nero,* it said.

"Do you have to get that?"

"No. I mean not yet . . . Honey . . ."

"Yes, Dad?"

"I will love you with all my heart for as long as I live, exactly the way you are. Whoever you are. Or turn out to be." He frowned. "That didn't come out right."

"I understand!" She hugged him. "Thanks, Dad. I love you, too."

"Thanks, honey," he said, really thankful. He hugged her tight.

"And don't tell Mom, promise? She'll have me in, like, a group therapy session in a second."

"God, no." His phone buzzed again. "Don't worry about that . . ."

"That's fine, Dad, take your business call. I've got to go. And if you can't get back in time just text me. I can get a ride with Rachel."

"Okay. Oh, and honey!"

She twisted back, door open, one leg out. "Yeah, Dad?"

"Until you get older, can you try, with girls . . . and definitely with boys, can you try to keep it, you know, let's say above . . ." He considered. ". . . the neck?"

"Haha, I love you, Dad."

She grabbed her duffel bag and jumped out the door, sprinting happily off to join her friends. He saw her hugging Rachel, the stocky blonde who got two goals in the last game. Was she the dyke? he wondered as he checked his phone.

Problem, the text said. *Truck. Meet me?*

"Fuck," Gio said. He would have to fight traffic back the other way now. He texted back: *Yes. Diner.*

Joe dropped by Circus City around five. It was a big place with a circus theme, obviously: the dancers on trapezes as well as poles, and peep shows in back made up to look like an old carnival. The club was open now but not busy yet, a good time to talk to the manager, a guy named Kit whom he'd seen around. And, yes, Kit was there in his office, door open, leaning back in his executive-style desk chair, chewing out some bartender in a bikini, bow tie, and red clown nose for being late. When he saw Joe in the doorway, he sent her back to work and waved him in. Joe shut the door.

"Hey, Joe, good to see you. Have a seat. Please tell me you're looking for a job."

"I don't know. Do you still make your bouncers dress like circus strongmen?"

"Yes. But, hey, my club's still open, right? And for you, lap dances and drinks are on the house."

"Tempting," Joe said. "But actually today I came by to ask a favor."

Kit sat up, his chair squeaking. "What kind of a favor?"

Joe took five bills from his shirt pocket and laid them on the desk. "The kind where I give you five hundred dollars right now, and you don't ask any questions. And then I give you another five later and you forget that this ever happened."

When Gio finally pulled into the diner's parking lot, a long twenty-five minutes later, his guy Nero was waiting, leaning on the hood of his Caddy and smoking a cigarette, which he tossed when he saw Gio. He came and leaned in his window, stinking of smoke.

"Gio, I'm sorry to bug you, but I figured you'd want to know. That truck full of knockoff bags, you know, Louis Vuitton, Gucci . . ."

"Yeah? What about it?"

"It got hit."

"Hit?" Gio frowned. "You mean *hit* hit, like hijacked?"

"Yeah." Nero reached for another cigarette. "Sorry."

That surprised Gio. He'd figured the cops had taken his truck—more pressure over the whole ISIS business—but robbed? People didn't usually rob Gio. Gio robbed them, and even then they were polite about it.

"Who was it?" he asked.

Nero shrugged. "They wore masks. But Tony said they talked to each other in some language that could be Mandarin."

"Tony speaks Mandarin?"

"No, but his kid is studying it in school. He wasn't sure, though. It could have been Cantonese. Sorry, Gio."

"That's okay, Nero." Gio understood what Uncle Chen was telling him, loud and clear. It was a warning shot. Soon, he'd be at war with the Triads, a criminal organization as deep as his own, and even if the other Italians lined up beside him, it promised to be bloody and costly. And the best way to avoid it was to hand over his old pal Joe.

23

Three hours later, Circus City was in full force. Strippers twisted on poles and trapezes, and once every half hour there was a lion-tamer act where one girl in a top hat with a whip and stool chased around two other girls in kitty ears and tails. The bartenders and servers dressed like clowns, and sure enough, the huge bouncer was in a leopard-skin caveman thing. Joe had to admit he made it work for him, posing by the door, muscles rippling.

Silly or not, the crowd loved it. Computer nerds, business guys, and car salesmen in loosened ties, construction guys, even a table of MTA workers—they were all here on Friday night, stuffing a big part of their paychecks into G-strings. Joe had left to get what equipment they needed earlier, then returned to set up, and Yelena had gone back to the dressing room to prepare, so by the time Shatz came in they were ready.

As described, he was a quiet type, slouchy, a little overweight, crooked tie. And Clarence was right about the redhead thing, too. When the DJ announced that Ruby was coming out, and Yelena appeared in nothing but black stockings, black panties, a black bra, heels, and a red wig, Shatz was galvanized. He couldn't look away. From where he was watching, in the shadows, Joe couldn't even see him take a breath.

You had to admit, she was definitely something to see. She must have been on some kind of gymnastics team back in Russia, or maybe all little girls took those classes over there. Anyway, she hooked Shatz like a trout and reeled him right in. When the DJ announced that Ruby would be appearing in one of the peep shows in back, he got right up like a zombie and walked. Actually, a couple of guys did, and one was a bit closer than Shatz, so Joe had to accidentally spill club soda on him to give Shatz the lead. Shatz headed down the hall to the booth with a sign saying RUBY, parted the curtains, and went in.

Inside, it was like an old freak show or house of wonders, with a stool and a fake wood door with a peephole at eye level. You bought tokens, ten bucks each, and fed them in the slot for five minutes. Shatz paid and pressed his eye to the hole. Nothing happened. He saw only blackness.

"One moment please," Yelena called out sweetly. "I'm not quite ready."

About ten precious seconds went by. Then the peephole opened and he saw her, posed with one foot propped on a chair. She moved and stretched, touching herself here and there, lifting her legs high in a balletic pose, then turning and bending again. She slipped the bra off carefully, and Shatz could hear himself breathe. Then, just as she was about to remove her G-string, the peephole shut. Token time. He eagerly slid another in. And she was back. Again she teased him, pulling the G-string up and down, letting him peek, then finally peeling it away, opening her thighs and letting him see. He was speechless, breathless, pretty much brainless, too. Then she spoke:

"If you want, I can open this door and let you in. But no tokens. Twenty dollars cash."

Shatz understood. For each token the girls turned in they got only six bucks, the house taking four as its cut. If he gave her a twenty, then she kept it all. He nodded, then remembered she couldn't see him and croaked hoarsely, "Okay."

She opened the door and he stepped through, as though through the looking glass. She plucked the twenty from his hand and, totally naked—well, except for shoes and stockings—she put him in the chair and eased herself onto his lap. He sat, petrified with pleasure, like a statue. She took his hands in hers.

"It's all right to touch me," she whispered, and placed his hands on her ideally round, firm ass. "I like when you squeeze me hard."

So he did it, he squeezed her ass hard, and she purred, moaning softly, and her breasts were just barely brushing his cheeks when suddenly it all went wrong.

"Hey! What the fuck is going on here?"

It was some guy in a T-shirt and jeans, looking angry. He pulled Ruby up by the arm and grabbed Shatz by the collar. "Who do you think you are, trying to fuck my girlfriend?"

"No! I'm not. I wasn't. She said—"

"She said what?" He turned to Ruby. "I warned you. This is it. You'll never work here again. And you . . ." He turned back to Shatz. "Get the hell out before I break your neck."

Shatz fled like a rabbit dropped from a dog's jaws. As soon as he was gone, Joe shut the fake wood door and removed the device that he'd placed over the peephole, while Yelena gathered her things. But she did not get dressed. They hurried out to the back storeroom where Juno was waiting.

"Did you get the iris print?" Joe asked him.

"Got it," Juno said, pointing to the laptop screen, where an image of Shatz's eye appeared. He'd downloaded it from the tiny camera whose lens had been over the peephole. "And now for the hands," he said, turning to Yelena. "Careful," he told her, picking up what looked like a flashlight. "Don't sit or touch anything. Just put your hands up."

She did so, raising her arms above her head. Joe turned off the lights, and when Juno turned his black light on, the prints of Shatz's hands appeared on both of her butt cheeks. The powder with which he'd dusted her before had taken the impression, invisible except under black light.

"Perfect," Juno said.

"The prints or my ass?" Yelena asked, looking over her shoulder.

"Both. Now hold still." He took two sheets of clear, sticky glassine and pressed them gently over each cheek.

"Are you going as fast as possible?" Yelena asked.

"Just being thorough." He peeled them off and checked. They held the prints. "Done," he said.

Yelena immediately removed the wig and pulled on her street clothes—normal underwear, jeans, a sweatshirt—while

Juno collected his equipment. Joe went and handed Kit five hundred dollars, then took them out the back door to where the Volvo sedan was parked. They all got in. Joe drove.

They went to a neighborhood bar in Yonkers where Don and Clarence were waiting in a back booth over beers. They looked up expectantly. Juno raised his arms in victory.

"Terrific, terrific," Clarence said, standing and shaking hands all around. "Any problems?"

"Nope. Joe's plan was smooth as silk," Juno said, sitting backward on a chair. Clarence slid in next to Don, and Yelena and Joe took the other side.

"What about me?" Yelena teased. "It was my ass on the line."

"You didn't let me finish," Juno went on. "Not even silk is as smooth as that ass. And I can testify, being the only one here to touch it."

Joe smiled at him. "You certainly took your time rubbing that fairy dust on her."

Juno shrugged. "Had to be thorough, man. We needed a good print."

"We're set," Clarence said. "Shatz will never make the connection. Even if the cops question him, he'll be too ashamed to breathe a word about this."

"Sorry to miss the show," Don said. "My compliments to you both." He held out a hand to Joe. "Very clever, mate. And, like you said, no mess."

Joe smiled and they shook. "Thanks."

"And let's keep it like that," Clarence said. "If we stick to the plan we can do this whole thing without getting bloody. In and out clean. That's why the client hired professionals." He stood, a little stiff but managing without the cane now, and took out his phone. "I'll let him know we're on for tomorrow. You guys order a drink on me." He waved the waitress over.

"My ass, my choice," Yelena said. "Vodka shots all around."

"Just coffee for me," Joe said.

Yelena scowled at him. "What's wrong, old man? Maybe you are all brains and no belly." She looked at the others. "Is that what you say in English?"

Don laughed. "I think you mean no balls."

Juno grinned. "I was going to order a cognac. But I guess I'll be having the vodka now, too."

"Fine," Joe said. "Make that an espresso."

At the hotel, Joe tapped on the door between his room and Juno's.

"Yo!" Juno called out, and Joe walked in. Juno was perched on the edge of his bed playing a video game. He had it running on one of the monitors he'd bought for use in the heist. "What's up?" he asked without looking away from the screen, where his avatar, clad in army gear, was shooting his way through a burning building.

"When you get a chance I need some tech support in here," Joe said.

"Trouble with the equipment for tomorrow?"

"I can't get HBO on the TV."

"Okay," he said. "Let me just kill these varmints." He pressed a button and a projectile shot across the screen, scattering body parts and eliciting pathetic screams as it exploded. A moment later, the building crumbled and the screen filled with rubble. "Damn it."

"What happened?" Joe asked.

"Roof collapsed."

Joe sat beside him, peering at the screen. "I think it was that pillar. In a compromised building, you can't use an RPG so close to a weight-bearing structure. You should have tossed in a shock grenade to stun them, then just moved in and taken them out."

"You play, Joe? I'm impressed you're a gamer."

"I was talking about real life."

"Right. Forgot about that for a sec." He handed Joe the controller. "Here, check this out."

"What? Me? I can't even get HBO on this thing."

Juno reset the game and a fresh avatar appeared, a superhero buff grunt in camo, dark-skinned and with a red headband holding up his Afro. "Now this is you. And these controls are, like, shoot, run, jump, kick, punch. Easy."

Joe struggled to get his man through the door of a building. "Damn it, I think it's broken."

"Nah, you're just a little spastic. Maybe you'd feel more at home in a white body? I can change it."

"Fuck off." Joe laughed, pushing Juno's hand away, then made it into the building and opened fire on the figures inside. "How's that? Better?"

"Except now you just killed your own captain. This ain't a Vietnam game."

"Does this thing have a PTSD flashback feature?" Joe asked, frantically pressing a button while his avatar jumped repeatedly and an enemy soldier shot him down. "Shit. My gun jammed."

"Nope, you were pressing the wrong button."

"Damn it."

"Have some patience." He went to the counter and grabbed some drinks. "Have a warm grape Snapple and try again."

Joe stood. "Call me a snob, but I believe it should be served cold." He grabbed the bucket. "I'll get ice."

He opened the door but hesitated when he saw Yelena in front of her room, down the hall, with Don beside her.

"Thanks, but no," she was saying, wriggling free as he tried to wrap a beefy arm around her. "I will teach you to wrestle another time. But now I need sleep. Big day tomorrow." She opened her door.

"You'll sleep so much better after another stiff drink," Don said, moving in, his face close to hers. "And a bloody brilliant orgasm."

"I know." Yelena smiled sweetly up at him. "That's exactly what I am going to have, in my room alone," she said, and slipped in, shutting the door. Joe took that as his cue and headed into the hall, swinging the bucket as he crossed paths with Don.

"Evening," he said.

Don grunted and walked to his room. His door slammed.

Joe got the ice, and when he returned, Yelena was watching him suspiciously from her doorway.

"Joe . . ." she said. He paused. "Why were you peeping at me and Don?"

"I was just getting ice. Me and Juno are having a Snapple."
She frowned in annoyance. "I thought maybe you were going to rescue me like the helpless damsel I am?"

Joe grinned at her. "Hardly. Though I admit I was a little concerned that you might kill him and I'd get stuck helping dump the body. He looks heavy." She smiled at that and he crossed the hall. "Good night," he said, and opened Juno's door.

"Good night," she said, and shut hers.

24

It was Saturday, so technically she was on her own time, personal business, but if anyone ever asked, Donna could say she was following a lead that turned up in the nightclub sweep. Or playing a hunch. Or maybe just scratching an itch. Which was closest to the truth? She wasn't sure, but after Mike picked up Larissa for their day together—soccer practice, then pizza and a movie—Donna drove to Queens, to Jackson Heights, the home of Gladys Brody, Joe's grandmother and only living relative. Actually, the only person who really knew Joe, as far as she could tell. Except Gio.

At the front steps of the old brick apartment building, she negotiated a dizzying crowd of kids on scooters, on bikes, kicking a soccer ball, playing hopscotch on a chalked outline. Then, in the courtyard, she walked a gauntlet of old biddies who sat in folding chairs, clucking away. Finally, beside the front door, a fat man in a wifebeater sitting on a milk crate and smoking a cigar watched her find 4A and buzz. No answer.

"Who you looking for?" he asked, exhaling cigar stink through his mustache, with a little BO mixed in, too. He had tufts of hair sticking out from his ears and from the sides of his armpits, as though there was just too much hair inside him to contain.

Donna smiled. "Gladys Brody. Do you know when she'll be back?"

He shrugged. "Who wants to know?"

She gritted her teeth but kept smiling. "I do. It's personal."

He stared back at her, thinking it over, and it seemed like a standoff till one of the biddies called out. "It's okay, Louie. I'll talk to the young lady."

Louie smiled, showing some real gold teeth and some smoke yellow, and pointed his cigar. Gladys was the littlest of the old ladies, like a dried shrimp with a carefully set white hairdo, electric-blue slacks, blue shoes, and a red-yellow-and-green blouse with parrots on it. She was smoking a Slim 100 and waving Donna over, asking, "What are you, hon?" At first Donna thought she meant racially until she followed up with: "Social worker or cop?" But then, before Donna could answer, she changed her mind, peering closer through her huge, round shades: "Nah, your suit's too good. You're either a lawyer or a Fed."

"Fed," she replied with a smile. "I'm Agent Donna Zamora, FBI." She showed her badge and then held out a hand.

Gladys shook it. "Good for you. I bet your mom is proud."

"She is, thanks."

"Don't let those guys push you around neither."

"I'll try."

"So what's the story? You here to arrest me?"

All the other ladies—all sizes, some in housedresses, some in casual wear like Gladys, one, good God, in a bikini, off by herself in a sunny spot with a foil reflector, roasting her already jerky-cured skin—turned and listened curiously.

"No, no, nothing like that." Donna chuckled awkwardly. "Just some questions. Maybe we should talk privately inside?"

Gladys shrugged, lighting a fresh cig from the butt of her last. "Here's good. I like to get some fresh air. But only in the shade. I burn easy. Not like you with that nice Spanish skin."

"Um, thanks . . ." Donna said, as Louie gallantly set his crate down behind her. She smiled again at the listening ladies and sat. "It's about your grandson, Joseph." She launched into her bullshit story about checking on last known whereabouts for all persons questioned in national security matters, but Gladys waved it off blithely.

"Who knows whereabouts with Joe? He's somewheres. I know that. Nowadays, he checks up on me, I don't check on him."

"You used to, though. When he was younger."

"Sure," she said, making it two syllables: *shoo-wah*. "I raised him from the time he was born."

"What about his parents?"

"Please. Parents? They were children, too. His mother was never any good. Just like her mother before her."

"You knew her, too?"

"Sure. The whole family. For years. Margie!" she yelled to an obese woman in a housedress and slippers, curlers in her hair. "You remember the Fabiolis?"

Margie nodded sagely. Gladys went on. "Italian. Not that I minded that. I love everybody." She waved her cigarette, taking in the whole scene. "All together. Italian, Jewish, white, Spanish . . ." She held there. "But what's true is true. Joe's mom, Regina Fabioli? She was a beauty, I'll give her that. But she drank. She ran around. And it caught up to her. She got sick and died when Joe was two."

"That's awful, to lose your mother so young. What about your son, Joe's father?"

"Him?" She brushed him off, flicking ash over Donna's trousers. "Useless."

"I know he had a lot of problems with the law," Donna said, trying to sound sympathetic. "He had a record as a thief and a grifter."

Gladys smiled. "Yeah, he was one of the best," she said, sort of wistful. "But money ran through him like water. Gambling. And the curse."

"The curse?" To the old ladies Donna knew, this meant your period.

"The Irish curse, hon. The bottle."

"Right."

"So he died, too, when Joe was six. After that it was just him and me." She shrugged. "I did my best. He had it rough. But he was sharp as a tack. Got into Harvard over all those rich kids. Took them all, too. That's why they kicked him out. They were embarrassed, 'cause he outsmarted them all. And then he went in the service."

"You must have been proud when he signed up."

"I was pissed. What kind of moron signs his freedom away? To fight in a war? It's like prison with people shooting at you. Voluntarily! But he did good there. He was a hero." She paused, smoking fiercely. "Not that they gave a shit." Then stomped her butt out. "Anything else you want to know?"

Donna blinked. "Just what he's up to lately? Who he spends his time with?"

Gladys grinned. "You mean girlfriends? You know, if I was still working as a fortune-teller, doing the crystal ball routine in the Village, I'd say you were the one who had a thing for him."

Donna laughed, but she could feel herself blushing. "Now, Gladys, you know that's crazy."

"Sure is, hon. That's why they call it love. Anyway, you want your cards read, you come back anytime."

After Larissa was asleep, Donna and her mom stayed up talking, drinking herbal tea, and eating cookies.

"Can I ask you something?" Donna got the milk from the fridge: better for dunking. "How come you never remarried?"

Donna's mom shrugged. "Why would I? I had you and I had a good job, with good benefits. What did I need a husband for?"

Her mom had worked in a booth for the MTA, underground for twenty-five years, first selling tokens, then Metro-Cards; giving tourists directions; and listening to riders' rage, their hot breath steaming the plastic, when the turnstile or card machines didn't work. It always amazed Donna how she could think that was a great job. But to her it was, and she had pressed Donna to work there, too. She'd wanted her to be a conductor, something she thought she couldn't do because of her accent. But Donna, she felt, had a lovely clear voice and a pure American accent. Donna thought she sounded like a girl from around the way, up in Washington Heights.

"And the same goes for you," her mom was saying. "With your job, you can take care of yourself and your daughter, thank God. Why would you want a husband to take care of, too?"

"But weren't you ever lonely without a man in your life?"

"Who said I was lonely? I said I didn't need a husband. I still needed a man."

"Mom!"

"And so do you."

"Mom!"

Her mom shrugged and dunked a cookie in Donna's milk.

"So when I was staying with Grandma . . ." Donna ventured.

"Of course. And you need a friend to visit you when Larissa is with me. Or with that crazy ex-husband of yours. Isn't there anybody interesting at work?"

"Not . . . really . . ." Donna said, though as she said it, an image popped unbidden into her brain.

"Come on, Donna, you can't fool me. I can tell from the way you said it. There is someone, isn't there?"

"No. Not really. I mean, it's impossible."

"Donna! A married man?"

"No, no, of course not. God, Mom, what do you think of me?"

Her mom shrugged, noncommittal.

"It's just . . . Well, he's definitely not the husband type, that's for sure."

"Is he exciting? Fun? Is he kind?"

Sorry. Donna thought about the apology before the shotgun went off. About him smiling as she put on the cuffs.

She smiled. "I don't really know him at all, but you know, I kind of think he is."

"And he must be handsome if you're blushing. Does he like you?"

"How would I know? Like I said, he's a stranger really. Just . . . someone I've crossed paths with on the job once or twice . . . maybe three times tops."

"Come on. You can tell. How does he look at you? How does he smile? It's in his eyes."

Donna dunked a cookie thoughtfully, let it dissolve on her tongue. "You know, the other day I was coming back from lunch with Andy and I thought I saw him."

"So? What happened?"

"Nothing. I'm not even totally sure it was him. But I was waiting to get a coffee and, for a second, I don't know, I kind of caught a glimpse of him right there in line behind me, like he was getting ready to talk to me and then didn't. Then when I looked he was gone. Just another figure in the crowd."

"That sounds like a bunch of nonsense. Just call him and say hi. See if he asks you out."

Donna laughed. "Actually, he did already. He asked me to his friend's wedding." She took another cookie.

"See? That's major. He likes you. Why didn't you go?"

"I couldn't."

"Why not?"

"Because of work. It was impossible. The whole idea is impossible. Just forget it."

"Okay, I will. But you won't. And you can say I'm crazy, but remember your mother knows things. I have a feeling about this one. It's not over between you two. There's more to come."

"Oh yeah? Does your psychic power tell you if it's going to be good or bad?"

"Nope. Not yet. Could be really good or really bad."

"Great. Thanks a lot." Her cookie, oversoaked, collapsed and sank into the milk. "Now look what happened." She took the spoon from her teacup, fished the cookie out, and ate it like soup.

25

The perfume job went off beautifully. Until it didn't.

They set Juno up in the back of the van on a small hill near the perfume company's headquarters. It was a quiet residential street that dead-ended into the rear of the company property, with big houses, big trees, and few streetlights, so a new, clean black van in the shadows would go unnoticed at least for a while. In the front was the entrance gate, the parking lot, the main doorway, guarded even now. The building itself was five stories, each but the first and fifth with a terrace around it, shaded by a French-style awning and filled with abundant plants. No doubt this was where employees took breaks or smoked, but Clarence told them they also grew the kind of scented flowers and plants that went into designing perfumes.

Clarence drove the Volvo around to the side of the property. This was the shortest distance between the ivy-covered fence and the building, where a side door opened near the dumpsters and A/C units. Don, Yelena, and Joe got out, all dressed in black with ski masks and gloves on, carrying AK-47s over their shoulders and light packs on their backs. Clarence would wait, ready to drive them away.

Don clipped the fencing and rolled it back. Then he spoke into the little mic attached to his earwig. "Okay, the fence is ready."

Juno opened the rear door of the van and let his drone fly out. It looked cool, buzzing over the houses and trees and then toward the office building, but he soon shut the door and turned to his monitor, as the drone quickly disappeared into the cloudy night. He had three screens lined up. One showed him what his drone saw, from the camera in its nose. The second showed him what the security cameras saw and sent to the guard at the front desk. He had already hacked into that system and could shut it down at will. And the third showed him the radar screen that the security company saw in its headquarters: a grid laid over a map of the property on which anything moving would register as a bright green shape. A tiny shape, like a squirrel or a bird, would be ignored. If a human-sized shape appeared off-hours, they would send the cops. That one was hardwired and he couldn't block it without finding and physically cutting the cables, but he didn't want to. His way, the folks at security HQ would think everything was chill. Juno smiled, watching his drone cam hover over the property while the radar screen didn't show shit. He pressed a few buttons, controlling the hardware installed in the drone.

"Okay," he answered into his own mic. "Radar jammed. You're good to go."

Don waved them in, keeping watch as first Yelena, then Joe ran through the hole in the fence and sprinted, heads down, for the side door. They stopped on either side of it, backs against the wall, and kept watch while Don ran up and ducked behind a dumpster.

"Door," Yelena said into her mic.

There was a click. "Door open," Juno answered, and she turned the knob. She nodded at Joe.

"Cameras now," he told Juno through the mic, and Juno shut off the security cameras.

"Cameras out."

At Joe's nod, Yelena swung the door open. Joe stepped in quickly, rifle ready. He was staring down an empty hall, with only a now-blind camera looking back at him. He waved at Yelena and she signaled Don, who sprinted inside. Yelena entered and shut the door. They were in. Phase one was complete.

Tom didn't mind working the midnight shift, even on weekends. First, he was prepping for the exams to get into the police academy and wear a real badge, so these quiet hours gave him time to study. Second, there was no boss around, not really; just his senior guards: Lou, who was taking a turn patrolling the outside grounds so that he could also sneak a smoke; and Barry, who was in the can and, considering that he had the new *Hustler* with him, would be in there a while.

So he wasn't really sure when the screens, which were supposed to show him the feed from the security cameras, first went dead. He had his head in a book and wasn't watching. But at some point he glanced up and saw the row of screens all full of static. Confused, he reached for his radio, but that was when he felt something cold and hard like a dead finger against the back of his neck.

"Don't do it," a man's voice said. "Don't do anything or you're dead. Understand?"

Tom froze. He couldn't believe what was happening.

The gun poked him harder. "Understand?"

"Yes, yes, I understand."

"Now put your hands flat on the desk and tell me where the other guards are now."

Tom told him.

"Good. Now with your right hand only, pick up your radio. The one in the men's room, that's Barry? Tell Barry to come take a look, that you have something weird to show him with the system, but don't make it sound serious. Understand?"

Tom nodded.

"Okay," the gunman said. "Go ahead."

"Hey, Barry, it's Tom. Over."

There was a long pause. "Yeah?"

"Could you come take a look at something? Nothing serious. My screen's being weird."

"Jeeze, can't it wait?"

"I don't know. Lou's out on patrol."

"Smoke patrol you mean. Funny, he ain't so eager in the winter. Okay. Be right out."

They heard a toilet flush. The gunman chuckled and Tom smiled, too, then remembered he was scared to death.

"Tom, that was great," the gunman said. "You're going to be fine. Now just stand up with your hands over your head."

He did so, and the guy quickly removed his gun and holster, his whole belt, then tied his hands behind him. He guided him gently to the floor, facedown.

"Now I'm going to tie you up, but it's just for a short time. Just stay down here for a little while till it's over. All right?"

Tom nodded, and the man quickly taped his legs together and pulled a cloth sack over his head, which freaked him out at first, but it was very thin and easy to breathe through. Really, Tom thought, for a guy committing armed robbery, he was pretty nice. He lay there quietly, behind his desk, trying to remember the penal code number for the crime of which he was now a victim.

After Joe got the young guard, Tom, bound and hooded, he nodded to the others. Yelena pressed herself to the wall by the corner leading to the hallway. Don took up a position behind the desk, watching out the front doors. As Barry, an older, heavyset man with a rolled-up magazine under his arm, came around the corner, still buckling his pants, Yelena tripped him easily and dropped him facedown on the ground.

He grunted and started cursing, but Joe pressed his rifle to the side of his head. "Don't move," he said. "Don't do anything or you're dead."

Once again, Joe and Yelena disarmed him and bound him, and Joe held the radio to his head and made him call Lou, the third guard, again for some minor reason. Then they hooded Barry, and together Joe and Don dragged him over next to Tom. They all ducked down behind the desk.

A few minutes later, Lou appeared at the front door. He entered his code, disabling the front door alarm, and came in. Don sprang up, rifle pointed at his chest. "Hold it," he barked. "Don't move a fucking finger or you're dead."

Once they had all three laid out together, they took their masks off and Don sat down behind the desk to keep watch, while Joe and Yelena went around the corner and into the hall.

"Elevator," Joe said, and Juno opened it. They got on and Yelena pressed five.

On five they crossed a small foyer to a large white sliding door, like the elevator, but just one panel. There was a terminal like an ATM beside it. Yelena pressed where the touch screen read, *Begin.*

"Hello," a calm female computer voice told them. "Please press your eye to the iris reader."

From her pack, Yelena took out a small tablet, which had the image of Shatz's iris on the screen, and pressed it to the camera on the terminal.

"Iris confirmed," the voice told them. "Please place your hands on the screen as shown."

Now Yelena removed two plastic sheets that had Shatz's handprints on them and pressed those against the outlines on the screen.

"Handprints confirmed. Welcome, Dr. Shatz."

The door opened.

"We're in the lab," Joe told the others over the earwig. Phase two was complete.

Phase three was the long one. Yelena crossed the large laboratory to a full-sized door set in the wall—the vault—and began unpacking her equipment. Even with the specialized tools she'd brought, it would take some time for her to cut through the multiple layers of titanium and steel.

Meanwhile, Joe stood watch in the doorway, guarding the empty hall, watching the motionless elevators, and looking over the lab. In most ways it looked like any other laboratory: lots of test tubes and beakers and burners on stainless steel tables, various machines and computers, a rack full of white coats. But there were also shelves, rows and rows of them, full of neatly labeled glass vessels sealed with rubber stoppers. Some held colored liquids, others plants or leaves or bits of wood, powdered spices, or bright seeds. Others held tobacco, dried fruits, even rubber, oil, or various molds. There was a whole row of furs and skins, and one of soils from around the world. There was sweat. There were glands. There was blood.

On the other side were the animals: several rows of little creatures in cages, mostly herds of rats and mice, swarming together in glass tanks, eating and shitting and, he supposed, reproducing as fast as they could. A large cage was full of fluttering pigeons. There were a few monkeys who began to screech and jump when Yelena came in but lost interest when they realized they were not going to get fed.

Off in one corner were a clear plastic wall and door, closing off a sterile space, with more machines and those pieces of equipment where you stuck your hands through the openings in yellow gloves. Zip-up work suits, booties, and caps were stacked beside the door.

Joe imagined Shatz and others in the white coats, adding a drop or dose of one thing to another. And then what? Sniffing it? How did they know what would be good together? And what about the scents that were good only to you, like the menthol smell of Vicks VapoRub melting into the humidifier that his grandmother put by his bed when he was sick, that he could hear sighing all night, and that meant safety and care? Or her cigarettes and hair spray, which meant love? Or the sizzle of dope cooking, which meant relief was on the way? Or how, when you shot the dull blank liquid into your vein, you instantly tasted it, scented it from the inside as it were, as if sense, like memory, surged up from within, not without. As if it were stored there, somewhere in the brain, or strung like beads along the nerves, or resting dormant in blood: dreams, nightmares, pleasure, pain, even love—all waiting for the right drop or mix of drops, the right potion to unlock them, the way these smells were trapped in jars, behind glass, sleeping until they were released into the world, for good or ill.

All in all it took an hour before Yelena, switching between various saws and a small torch, stopped and called Joe over. "Come help," she said, removing her safety goggles. "This will be heavy."

Joe pulled out his knife and unfolded the blade. He stuck it in the edge of the large, chest-high section she had cut, and slowly pried it open, moving side to side. When it had eased out enough to grip, they both got their hands on the corners and pulled. Made of dense metals, it felt like a panel of stone, or a rough-hewn tombstone awaiting a name. Finally it fell forward, and they let it drop with a bang, cracking the tile floor. Yelena had cut a small door inside the larger door. Now Joe realized what she was—the way she moved; the way she watched, half wary, half wicked; her expertise in burglary. She was a cat.

"Nice work," he told her, and stepped through.

She smiled proudly, behind Joe's back, but then erased it. "We are in the vault," she told the others. Phase three was done.

Following the instructions Clarence had given them, they ignored the many drawers and shelves of vials and went directly to a glass cupboard in the back. It contained just four vials, each a small glass tube set in a larger, specially formed plastic case, like a precious jewel in a custom-made gift box. Each of the cases was sealed and numbered on the front. They found the one that matched the long number Joe had copied out on his hand. It was a few ounces of yellow liquid, like a urine sample.

"So that's what a million dollars looks like," he said, and handed it to Yelena, who put it in her pack. They left everything else and walked out.

Joe checked the hall, then nodded to Yelena. She spoke into her mic. "We got it. We're coming out."

"Clear down here," Don said.

"Clear," Juno said.

"All clear here and ready to go when you are," Clarence said from the car.

As they got back in the elevator, Yelena and Joe couldn't help finally grinning broadly at each other. Joe put out his hand and they shook. As the doors opened downstairs, he stepped out first, leading the way, and they proceeded back down the hallway toward the entrance hall. Then, as he turned the corner, everything went black.

Part III

26

"Joe . . . Joe . . ."

He wasn't out for very long. As soon as he realized he was alive and on the floor with his wrists bound behind him, his next thought was the law. But, no, he was still in the building, in the lobby, and he could hear Yelena beside him, trying to wake him up.

"Joe!" She kicked him sharply in the butt.

"Okay, I'm up." He tried to turn his neck. "What happened?"

"Don," she said.

"How long ago?"

"Maybe a minute. He knocked you out from behind, then had the gun on me. I didn't get the chance to kill him. Yet."

"Okay," he said. "Hang on."

Joe worked his hands down to his waist and, using the tips of his fingers, eased his knife from his back pocket. He unfolded the blade outward and wriggled back toward her.

"See if you can cut your hands free." He waited, hearing her wriggle and grunt. His head was throbbing, and it was sore on top, but he didn't think he was bleeding. Don had done a nice clean job of knocking him out.

Yelena got free and sat up, grabbing his knife and cutting his wrists loose before freeing her own ankles. She gave back the knife and Joe cut the tape from his legs.

He jumped up, got his gun, and checked that it was still loaded. Across the lobby, by the front desk, he could see the three guards still lying there, though they'd moved a bit and one, Tom maybe, was squirming like a worm on a hook.

"Which way?" he asked Yelena.

"Back like we came," Yelena said, and they ran, yelling into their mics but hearing nothing. Joe jumped over the guards.

"Help!" Tom yelled. "Police!" Barry was rolling back and forth now, trying to work up enough momentum to sit. Lou was snoring.

They ran back down the hall where they had come from and paused at the door. Joe looked at Yelena and she nodded. He turned the knob and pulled it open, and they both went through, rifles ready. That's when the flashlights shone in their faces. Before they blinded him, however, Joe could just catch a glimpse of Clarence in the escape car, driving away. Then someone opened fire, strafing the building above them. Chipped concrete rained down, and they jumped back inside and shut the door.

Joe and Yelena ran down the hall yet again and into the lobby. By now Barry was on his feet, still bound and hooded. He took a few hops and fell over. Lou was still out and Tom had squirmed all the way to the front doors, through which Joe could see cops approaching. It looked to be SWAT, in armor and visors, with headlamps shining and weapons drawn.

"Elevator," he called to Yelena, and they ran back down the other hall and got in again and pressed five.

"Goddamn that coward Clarence," Yelena said. "I will kill him, too."

The elevator opened, and Joe saw from the lit numbers that another elevator was approaching. They hurried back into the lab, this time closing the door behind them. It clicked and a red light turned on above.

"Door locked," the calm female voice told them. "Security system engaged."

Joe took a deep breath. They were safe for the moment, behind a fireproof steel door that only Shatz and the other two could open.

"It's Juno I wonder for," Yelena said as they began rummaging around the lab, knocking stuff over as they searched for something useful. "Do you think the cops got him?"

"I don't know," Joe said, as the monkeys jeered. "But doesn't this response seem like overkill for a perfume robbery?"

Joe could hear the SWAT team banging on the door. SWAT wasn't sent in first because they were the smartest, but still, they'd figure it out soon enough. What if Shatz was already here, about to be brought up?

Yelena kicked a table over in frustration. "Nothing."

"Okay," Joe told her. "Let's try the roof."

They went to the emergency exit, and while Yelena held her gun ready, Joe swung it open. The alarm went off, and the red exit light began to flash. Now the lab door was completely sealed, even from Shatz, and the security company would have to come and reset it. It also meant they had burned that bridge behind them. They went out onto the roof, easing the door back to cut the light, dropping into crouches. Darting to the edge and peeking over, they could see police vehicles in the parking lot and sirens turning. Cop flashlights dotted the dark grounds, but most of the activity now seemed centered in front. Joe ran around the perimeter of the building, checking things out, while Yelena watched the door.

"I'm thinking maybe they think they've got us trapped, so they're not hunting on the grounds so much," Joe said when he got back.

"I'm thinking they are right," she said. She looked over the edge, then back at him.

"I've got one idea," she told him. "But I don't think you will like it."

"Does it get us on the ground alive? Then I like it."

"That depends. How flexible are you?"

They held hands and jumped. First Joe had yanked out a cable that ran across the roof and then down the side of the building. He wound the end around his waist, and then he and Yelena climbed onto the ledge and jumped, bouncing onto the awning and then sliding down to crash onto some bushes, while the cable jerked free behind them.

"Okay?" Yelena asked him. He was a little scratched up from the bushes.

"So far," he said, and climbed the next railing.

He took her hand and they jumped. Again they slid, this time hitting an umbrella over a table, which broke their fall but also dropped Joe onto a chair that knocked his already sore head. Yelena, as expected, landed light as a cat.

The third awning didn't go as smoothly. They jumped just the same, but this time they somehow hit the supporting structure and the awning collapsed, falling sideways and dumping them onto the terrace like a slide. They tumbled out, bumping and cursing, but they were down now, just two stories above the ground. The next jump was bigger, though, and there was no awning to break their fall.

Joe unwound the cable he'd collected and tied one end to the heavy leg of a bolted-in bench. He yanked it tight. Next he wound the cord around his waist and tied the other end to the back of Yelena's belt.

"Ready?" he asked.

She nodded. He braced himself, foot on the edge, and pulled hard.

"You better not drop me," she said.

"I won't," he told her.

She slid herself carefully over the side. When the slack ran out, Joe pulled back, leaning all his weight into it, letting the cord play out slowly as Yelena dangled, like a spider descending, swaying this way and that, rappelling off the wall and letting herself settle finally on her toes. When Joe felt the cord relax and her weight come off it, he leaned over and peered down. She waved.

Yelena untied the cable from her belt, and Joe used the loosened slack to wriggle his waist free. Then she secured her end to the A/C unit. Joe took his belt off and, sitting on the ledge, cinched it tight around the cable. He grabbed on with both hands and eased himself over.

At first the cord jerked sickeningly as the slack pulled and he dipped. But then it pulled taut and he slid, hanging from the belt and kicking his legs, till Yelena caught him at the bottom. He freed his belt while she cut the cable so it fell back against the dark building, then they ran through the opening they'd made in the fence, where Clarence should have been waiting.

Joe and Yelena ran full speed now, away from the building and into the sleeping neighborhood around it. Soon, they knew, the police would find the cable or open the door and realize that they were running, and then the real hunt would begin. The task now was to cover as much distance as possible before that.

So they ran, turning down streets to avoid streetlamps and hiding behind bushes or in driveways to avoid cars. About five blocks from the lab, they saw a cop car roll by with its searchlights on, and they dived into the gutter to hide behind a parked car. Finally they passed a driveway that had what Joe wanted.

"Wait," he called in a loud whisper. "Over here." He ran back to where the old Lincoln was parked, white with rust along the bottom. "Keep an eye out," he told Yelena, and then, covering his rifle with his ski mask, he busted open the small triangular side window. He reached through, straining, and after a couple of tries, he lifted the door lock button. He slid in and opened the passenger door for her. Then he got his knife out and jammed it hard into the ignition. He turned, hoping the battery wasn't dead in this old heap. The engine sputtered, then roared to life. With the lights off, he put the car in reverse and backed out, then sped a few blocks more before turning the headlights on and reverting to normal speed. Ten minutes later they were back on the highway, heading toward New York City.

"Where to?" he asked.

"I don't know," she told him. She lit a cigarette. "You got any friends to hide us?"

"Not at the moment," he admitted.

She blew smoke out. "I do. In Brighton Beach."

"Sounds good," Joe said. "Just do me a favor. Open the window if you're going to smoke. And put your goddamn seat belt on."

27

Don and Juno torched the van in a vacant lot in the South Bronx. Juno hated to see all that beautiful equipment, especially his stealth drone, going up in smoke. But there was a lot about this job he was starting to hate, including his new partner, Don.

Juno hadn't planned on the double-cross. He was sitting in the van, his control center. Everything was going off like clockwork, like a goddamn Swiss watch. Joe and Yelena had just reported that the perfume was in hand, and Juno was all smiles. He liked her. What's not to like about a chick who can pole dance and crack safes? He was waiting for them to exit and for Clarence to report that they were driving away, at which point Juno would close up shop and drive the van to meet them. Then everything went silent. Juno waited. He checked in and no one answered but Clarence, who was still standing by. He kept waiting, while a couple of more excruciating minutes dragged themselves by like hours. Then the van door opened and he almost jumped out of his skin. It was Don.

"Holy fuck, man, you scared the shit out of me."

"I've got the perfume," he said, scrambling in. "Let's go."

"What do you mean? Where are the others? You're supposed to be with Clarence."

"The plan went wrong. We have to move," Don said, sitting in the passenger seat.

"But don't you think—"

Don pointed the rifle at him. Juno was unarmed. "What I think, mate, is you have two options: rich or dead. Which is it?"

Juno shrugged. "Rich is better."

"Agreed. Now turn the security system back on."

"But . . ." Juno was going to protest, but there was no point, he realized. He did it. In seconds the police and the security company would be alerted. In minutes probably there'd be cops. There was no turning back.

"Now drive," Don said, and Juno drove.

Don directed him into the South Bronx somewhere. This was all foreign territory to Juno. He was Brooklyn born and raised. A smart, nerdy kid, he had learned to live by his wits. Don't rat. Never burn a friend. But he'd also learned that survival came before everything else. It was a dog-eat-dog world. And anyway, since when were these folks his friends?

By the time they got to the lot, Don had started to relax, at least enough to put the rifle up. He didn't trust Juno. He didn't even care for blacks generally—not in a racist way; he just didn't trust them. Then again he didn't trust anyone. But he didn't need to. He knew Juno was bright. Juno would see that there was no turning back now. They were together, cut off from the others. Clarence would happily kill them both if he could but would put the job first and make a deal. Joe and Yelena were busted or dead. Juno's only way out was to stick with Don now. So he would.

Don had Juno park and then get into the nondescript Toyota Corolla he'd left discreetly parked on the sidewalk. He got the C-4 he had stashed in the trunk and quickly rigged the van. They took off as the van exploded, burning up all the evidence and melting Juno's toys.

28

Joe was exhausted. He'd been trained to go long periods without rest or food, and also to snatch what sleep he could, in trucks or transport planes or holes in the dirt. But he wasn't accustomed to this lifestyle anymore, and the tension and bad dreams kept him from really getting much rest at all. They left the stolen car, engine running, by a video arcade in East New York where Yelena knew kids hung out, taggers and stoners who would take it for a joyride or sell it for a quick buck. Then they took a gypsy cab to Neptune Avenue, rifles wrapped in a picnic blanket they'd found in the car. Now they were in Russian territory. Yelena led him down a few more streets, to the boardwalk, which was still bustling on this warm summer night. Families sat around platters of smoked sturgeon and herring, and men in shorts and flip-flops drank vodka and played cards. Kids were kicking a soccer ball around and riding their bikes and scooters, wheels thumping rhythmically over the planks in the boardwalk. Beyond the lights, the beach glowed in the moonlight, and beyond that, the ocean, invisible and eternal, swept darkly in and out. They entered the vestibule of a building. Yelena buzzed and was immediately let in; she'd called ahead.

The apartment was a comfortable mess: an open kitchen as you entered, then a dining and living room with sliding glass doors that opened onto the terrace, beyond which you could hear the waves. The shades were drawn. Bedrooms to each side. The place was crammed with upholstered armchairs, leather couches, a wooden dining table covered in a woven white tablecloth and heaped, like every other surface, with books, Cyrillic newspapers, overflowing ashtrays, and empty teacups. A large samovar sat on a sideboard. A chessboard between two club chairs held a half-fought game. Shelves groaned with books and more stacks of paper. In the midst of it all stood an old Russian man with a fringe of white hair, in linen trousers, a crumpled white shirt, and slippers. A cigarette burned in his mouth.

The man kissed Yelena on the cheeks three times, then shook hands with Joe, saying, "Welcome," then immediately launched into a long Russian dialogue with her, at the end of which, with a flurry of nods and smiles, he led them into a bedroom, furnished in the same heavy style, with a big bed, a headboard, a mirror-topped chest of drawers, a dressing table, chairs, end tables, rugs. He gestured to Yelena, and she stood straight-shouldered before a rare patch of empty white wall. He adjusted a lamp, then pulled a small digital camera from his pocket and snapped.

"Now you," Yelena told Joe, and he stood in the same spot. The man took the picture and, muttering in Russian, went out. He returned seconds later with a bottle of vodka on a tray with two shot glasses. Yelena said something and he looked at Joe, laughed heartily, and went out again, shutting the door behind him.

Joe looked at her quizzically. She shrugged. "I told him you don't drink. He thought I was joking." She slid the lock shut and leaned a chair against the door, so that it would fall loudly if the door was opened.

"I thought you said you trusted this guy?" Joe asked her.

"I said he would never call the cops. He barely speaks English anyway, and in Russia no sane person calls the police." She pulled a Beretta from her ankle holster, checked it, and slid it under a pillow. "We are reasonably safe here," she told him. Then she grabbed the bottle and took a slug.

"Give me that," Joe said, and took the bottle from her. She watched while he took a deep drink. He grimaced. It burned like hell going down, but he needed to sleep. Almost immediately, he felt the burn become liquid warmth in his belly, then spread through his tensed body and eventually, he hoped, to his brain. He drank again and handed it back to her. She smiled.

"Bravo. Now you are like Russian." She went into the bathroom and turned the shower on full blast, then came out as the steam began to gather. "Next thing any Russian would do," she told him, "is get in some hot steam and water."

With the same quick, feline movements she had used to break the safe and leap from the roof, she peeled her clothes off and left them in a pile. As she reached back to unsnap her bra, Joe noticed something he hadn't seen before, when she was naked, or seemingly naked, in the club: tattoos. There were two eight-pointed stars, inked in black, on her upper chest, one in each of the shallows under her clavicle. As he stared in surprise, she grabbed the bottle, toasted him, took another slug, and carried it into the bathroom, leaving the door open. And when she turned, Joe glimpsed more ink: a large Madonna and child down the center of her back, finely lined and shaded in black, and a skull and a dollar sign each riding a hip as she wriggled out of her briefs and stepped into the scalding hot shower.

Smiling thoughtfully, he sat down and quickly took off his sneakers, then pulled off his T-shirt and jeans. Now in his boxers and socks, he stretched, then leaned over to peel his socks off, groaning as a sharp pain stabbed his back where he'd landed on the broken awning. Thanks to the vodka, his sore head was a bit better, as long as he moved slowly, but still, he thought he'd stretch his back for just a second before he joined Yelena.

By the time Yelena got out of the shower and came back wrapped in a towel, he was laid out, snoring away.

"Sweet dreams, Joe," she said, and taking the bottle with her, she slid under the sheets and rested her head on the pillow, under which she felt the reassuring shape of her gun.

29

Adrian was definitely not pleased, but it was Heather whom Clarence was really afraid of. At least right now. Adrian—tall, thin, with those icy eyes—was a stone cold killer, some kind of psychopath probably, but he was under control. That was his thing. When Clarence called and told him something had gone wrong, he didn't even raise his voice, just asked him to please come over. And when Clarence told him what happened, he barely blinked, just frowned slightly as if his soup was cold. Of course, Clarence knew very well that Adrian would just as soon cut his heart out as talk to him, and would do so with the same easy smile, or cold-soup frown. But he'd at least think it over first, hear him out. Heather, the blond pixie, who looked like a girl from a shampoo commercial, might just pull a gun out and fill him with bullets before he even sat down. Luckily, she just glared.

Adrian pointed to a chair. Clarence sat down, feeling a bit relieved. He was also reassured by the fine view of the High Line from the apartment that Heather had rented, via the Internet, through one of her many fake IDs and accounts. The keys had been FedExed to their last fake address, and in the large, crowded building, with shopping, food, and parking on the lower floors, they came and went unnoticed—just another rich, handsome couple in a rich, handsome neighborhood. No way would they murder him in front of a wide-open window, in full view of the other rich people and a thousand tourists traipsing back and forth over the High Line, the onetime abandoned highway and train track transformed into a long riverside park that passed right beneath them. Exhibitionists sometimes fucked in the windows of the nearby hotel on purpose—or, as the more cynical said, they were hired to pretend by the management—so that the folks down there could see. Whatever their twists, Heather and Adrian were not exhibitionists: if they were going to slaughter Clarence, they'd close the blinds. Clarence took a breath and told them what happened.

"Everything went perfect. The plan was solid. We would have gotten away clean, but they pulled a double-cross."

"Who?" Adrian asked.

"That limey merc, Don; and the kid, Juno."

"You're sure?"

"Don didn't pass me, so he escaped a different way, most likely out the front gate. The guards were all tied up, the cameras were down. Then someone turned the security system back on behind him. That had to be Juno."

"And the other two?" Heather asked, eyes glittering fatally at him. "The Russian and your pal, the one who saved you from your last fuckup?"

"Busted, probably. I took off when the police showed. Though if anyone could slip through, I guess they could."

"You took off and left them," Heather sneered.

"Was that wise?" Adrian asked. "We could have learned a lot from them."

"I had to," Clarence pleaded. "If I got caught, then what? The whole operation is down. I'm the only link with them, remember? Like you wanted." Clarence took out his phone and showed it to them. "Now, whoever has it, they will call me. How else are they going to get paid?"

There was a pause. Heather sniffed, but she crossed her legs and sat back, seemingly no longer about to spring at him. Adrian looked thoughtfully at the phone. Clarence stood.

"You mind?" he asked, gesturing at the kitchen. "I could use a drink."

Adrian nodded. "And they still have no idea what they really stole?" he asked Clarence's back as Clarence got the vodka from the freezer and filled a short glass with rocks.

"None. How could they?" Clarence explained as he poured. "And anyway, these are pros. You think if they knew thousands of people were going to die, they ever would have taken the job?"

Adrian considered that. "Not for that price, I imagine."

"No," Clarence said, thinking he should be getting a hell of a lot more himself, but not saying it. "Stealing some kind of deadly Frankenvirus would definitely cost you more than a bottle of perfume. Don maybe would've gone for it. The Russian girl, I don't know. She's hard to figure. But that guy Joe? I know his type. He would have left me dead on the highway if he thought for a second I was getting him mixed up in shit like this." He took a big sip. "Don't worry, one way you can know for sure that they don't know is I'm still alive."

Adrian laughed. "Then you have nothing to worry about, either."

Heather waved her nail file at him. "As long as they don't get curious and decide to open the vial and take a sniff."

"Right," Adrian said. "Then the whole neighborhood dies."

Heather and Adrian met at Stanford, got engaged during junior year, and just after they graduated—he magna cum laude with a 3.9 GPA, she summa cum laude with a 4.0—they married on a warm spring day. They were both pretty, both brilliant, and both orphans, of a sort: his parents had died when he was a young child; her father had had a heart attack while having sex with his mistress, and her mother had been back and forth between rehabs and psych wards since Heather was born. He'd been sent to school on a fellowship; she'd merely dipped into her inexhaustible trust fund.

But despite all the obvious parallels, losses, and gifts that made them seem like the perfect pair to outsiders, it was an even deeper element that fused them together: commitment. Heather had always known there was something different about her, something "wrong" she supposed, or would suppose if she had any sense of right and wrong. She was diagnosed early with possible antisocial personality disorder, the new, softer term for sociopathy, but with a family lawyer assuming guardianship whenever her mother was declared incompetent, and a nanny and doctor overseeing her education and care—in other words, employees—she was pretty much free to grow up wild, a kind of deluxe feral child, and with her intelligence, athleticism, and pretty smile, she moved easily on to girls' boarding school, the perfect training ground for a young sadist.

But she lacked self-knowledge, and, alternately indulging and repressing her own dark urges, she remained a victim of herself, until she met Adrian. Despite their utterly incongruous backgrounds, he was exactly like her. Exactly. Except for one thing. He had a cause around which to focus his energy: the destabilization, corrosion, and eventual destruction of American liberal democracy.

A big goal. But part of the discipline that Adrian had taught her was that people like him, like them—warriors in the service of a cause—thought not in terms of weeks or years or election cycles, but in centuries, in epochs. They were creating a future. And really, when you looked at the state of things here in the United States, that big goal was a lot more realistic, and a lot closer, than even the most optimistic fanatic could wish. Given the chance, America would destroy itself. All they were doing was helping.

30

When Joe woke up, Yelena was holding his hand tight in both of hers. "Joe," she was saying softly to him. "Joe, wake up."

"What's wrong?" he asked, sitting up abruptly and looking around. It was dark in the room. The moon had come out and was there in the window, and he could hear the surf. His body, he realized, was slick with sweat.

"Nothing," Yelena said, her voice different from before. She spoke softly and soothingly, in a whisper. "You were screaming in your sleep."

"Oh . . ." He sat back. His breathing slowed. She brushed his forehead, smoothing his hair back.

"Do you remember what was the dream?" she whispered.

"No," Joe lied.

Her fingers traced the scars on his side and the long one that ran down his thigh.

"It's okay," she said, shifting so that her arm was around him, holding him against her. He felt her soft skin against his skin; he felt her slow breath rising and falling. "You don't have to say if you don't want."

He said nothing, and after a little while, they fell back to sleep like that.

31

Donna wasn't sure how she was going to spend her free Sunday morning, while Larissa was at her dad's place. Maybe go for a run. Maybe read the paper for once. Maybe just sleep. She definitely hadn't planned on waking up at seven and rushing to work.

Saturday night had been a dull dinner with an awkward guy, a tax attorney she'd met on a dating site. He was fine—smart, nice looking, polite—but there was no real spark, and they both seemed to know it. He invited her back to his place for a drink but seemed almost relieved when she declined. That was the problem—guys in law enforcement were too much work and she'd sworn off them after the divorce. Regular guys either bored her or, even if she liked them, seemed never to really relax around her. Maybe men were intimidated knowing she could kick their asses. Maybe it was the gun strapped to her side, which one dude had accidentally touched when trying to get to second base. "Sorry!" he'd cried, as though afraid she'd shoot him. That was that. He didn't try again.

So she was most definitely alone, in bed and in the apartment, when her phone went off at 7:02 and she answered in a voice thick with sleep. It was an emergency, all hands on deck. Last night, in Westchester, someone had broken into a top secret government facility and stolen some top secret shit.

The next time Joe woke, the sun was out and Yelena was gone from the bed. He got up and looked out the window. A few people were swimming already, chopping their way through the waves. Others ran on the beach. The old Russians sat on the boardwalk benches. Someone was flying a kite.

Joe could smell coffee, and though the bedroom door was shut, the lock was off and the chair was set to the side, so he pulled his clothes on and went out to find Yelena curled up on the couch, sipping coffee, while the old man sat beside her in a chair, smoking.

"Good morning," he said in his thick accent, and poured Joe some coffee.

"Thanks," Joe said, waving off the offer of sugar or cream. He sat in an armchair and sipped.

"Look, he's done already," Yelena said. "I told you he was the best."

The night before, in the car, after she'd called to arrange this lodging, she'd also had Joe make up a couple of fake names, which she'd texted over. Now she proudly displayed the results: a fake driver's license in one of the names and a passport in the other, along with credit cards for both. Yelena had her own matching set. "I told him we'd pay later, after we get our money. He knows I will come back."

Joe inspected the work. He smiled at the old man. "These are excellent. As good as I've ever seen."

She translated, and the old man, clearly pleased, laughed it off. He said something in Russian, then lit another smoke. Yelena translated: "He says that he apologizes. These fakes were the best he could do right now. If he had a week, he could get you the real thing."

32

Gio's people hit Uncle Chen back on Sunday morning. Gio didn't really have a choice. War with the Triads was the last thing he wanted, but he couldn't let anyone take what was his and go unpunished. Still, much like angry nations that began with gestures, such as firing rockets over ships, then moved on to sanctions and trade wars, his response to the truck was nonviolent, mostly.

On Canal Street, hidden behind a storefront selling tourist junk, was a large, brightly lit white room where customers, almost all female, eagerly paid cash for expert copies of high-end designer bags, wallets, belts, and other leather goods by Louis Vuitton, Hermès, Gucci, Kate Spade, and others. The merch was heaped on folding tables where salespeople, mainly Chinese women of any age, from teenagers sipping bubble tea to grandmas in slippers, hawked it to a roaring crowd of ladies of every race and background, from businesswomen, lawyers, and executives to moms and daughters shopping for gifts to gangs of girlfriends who came in from Brooklyn or Long Island or Jersey, all drawn by the dazzle of a bargain. In the rear, past the long line waiting for the two washrooms (one was marked MEN, but not today), a stairway led to the basement. African men, mostly from Nigeria and Ghana, were packing up huge piles of goods and wrapping them in colorful blankets that they would unfold to sell on street corners and in train stations, bus depots, and parks, then refold in a flash when the cops appeared and melt into the crowd.

A couple of older Chinese men walked the floor like pit bosses, overseeing the flow of cash, and some young toughs stood by the door, mostly on the lookout for cops and to make sure no one tried to jump any of their customers, although that was unlikely: this was Triad territory, and while other groups might fight among themselves like alley cats and wild dogs, the Asian gangs were known for running a tight, smooth operation and keeping the mess off the streets.

But not this Sunday. Around eleven, right at the height of the pre-brunch sales swarm, Gio's guys moved in. Muscle-wise it was no big deal. A van backed into the alley beside the store, while a couple of cars full of bruisers double-parked outside, effectively controlling the exits. Two guys went in quickly and tackled the doormen. Then a platoon of masked dudes stormed through, yelling and waving bats, kicking over tables. One guy fired a gun into the roof. Panic erupted. The crowd rushed for the door, though an impressive number of these square ladies held armloads of swag as they ran. It was a free-for-all. Meanwhile, Gio's team opened the side door and started loading the van, in recompense for what he lost in the hijack. In fact, some of it appeared to be the same stuff.

Then, distracted by the mayhem and lulled into com-
placency, Gio's boys let their guard down, underestimat-
ing their adversaries—always a mistake. An angry granny
hauled off and smacked a guy in the head with a stool.
Another guy got kicked in the balls. Then the Africans,
hearing the uproar, came up to see what was happening
and jumped in on the Chinese side. A full-on brawl began,
fists and bats flying. Then sirens were heard and everyone
fled, declaring an instant truce while running side by side
from the law. The police caught no one, except some shoppers who were trapped and released, but the secret store
was shut down, the merchandise was seized, and the whole
party played on the local news.

A big success for Gio, Nero assured him, and all the guys
laughed their asses off while he told the story in the back of
the ice-cream truck warehouse where Gio held a quick meeting before heading over to Caprisi's, the family restaurant,
for Sunday dinner. But all he felt was stress, frustration over
the past, and dread of the future—the very things his wife
told him to avoid and let go of. To breathe through, as in
yoga. To release, so that he could stay centered, here, now,
in the present.

But it didn't work. At dinner he had no appetite, which
did not go down well with his mother, and he lost his temper with the kids, which pissed off Carol. Afterward, when
he told her he was going to swing by the gym for a boxing
workout, she urged him to go for once. It was that bad. He
texted Paul, who was at the movies, but who answered that
they could meet in an hour. Gio hated people who answered
texts at the movies, and sometimes he had to restrain himself

from snatching their phones from their hands and crushing them underfoot . . . but in this case he was relieved.

The gym was a good cover. For one thing, one of his properties did actually lease space to a boxing gym, and it made sense as a place he might go after work or on the weekend. And it explained why he came home bruised.

33

Joe and Yelena had brunch on the boardwalk, and since their Irish credit card was paying, she ordered them caviar blinis, a sturgeon platter, and smoked salmon with eggs. The food was delicious, and for a while neither spoke as they both wolfed it hungrily down. She ate nearly as fast as he did, and just as much. Families filled the tables around them, and a constant stream of people trooped by: parents holding kids by the hand as they headed toward Coney Island for rides and hot dogs; teenagers smoking and trying to jump the benches on skateboards; old Russian men heading to the water, carrying their hard round bellies before them, or heading back, water dribbling behind them as they sat to dry in the sun; young women in shorts and sandals or jeans and heels, stepping carefully over the planks. Clutches of old women chattered on the benches. A group of younger men leaned and smoked along the railing, some muttering into phones, others with their eyes closed against the sun. They took their shirts off, and Joe noticed their tattoos.

"I like your tattoos," he told Yelena. "You got them in Russia?"

"You noticed? I didn't think you even looked at me last night." She signaled a waiter for two coffees and then lit a smoke.

Joe smiled. "Oh, I noticed plenty. But I'm not used to drinking. Or jumping off roofs. What can I say? You wore me out."

Now she smiled, too. "A lot of men say that."

"Somehow that doesn't surprise me. But the tattoos did. You covered them with makeup for the club?"

She nodded, thanking the waiter in Russian as the coffee came. "I wanted to blend in, you know? To be less identifiable. And maybe someone there can read Russian tattoos."

"Even with makeup and a wig, I doubt you ever blend in."

She laughed, smoke billowing up. "Sorry. It is too late for flirting now, my friend. You had your chance."

Joe laughed with her. He drank his coffee, and as the waiter passed, he handed him his card. "Well then," he told her, "as your fake husband, let me make it up to you and take you shopping."

They rode the train into the city and hit the stores. Joe bought a pair of jeans, some T-shirts, underwear, and socks— not from a package this time—and a black suit, along with a couple of white button-downs and two ties, one black, one blue. Yelena bought a dress, jeans, T-shirts, underclothes, and designer running gear and sneakers. They bought tooth- brushes, toothpaste, deodorant, and other toiletries, and Yelena got a hairbrush. Then they got suitcases to carry it all and checked into a downtown hotel, someplace midrange and midsized, using the same credit card and posing as an Irish couple on their honeymoon. Joe managed a passable accent based on his paternal great-uncle, good enough to fool the friendly, not terribly bright young woman who worked the Sunday shift. Yelena just smiled.

They unpacked, changed, and threw their old clothes into the trash on the way out. Joe had on clean jeans and a fresh T-shirt. Yelena wore a blue cotton dress that showed off her shoulders. They went into separate banks and took cash advances on the Irish cards. Then they went on the hunt for Clarence. He seemed the logical starting point. Don was just a name: some British prick named Don. Juno was a kid. Clarence was a local and a longtime pro, and he had been the contractor who hired the whole string for the heist, which implied he knew people and was known.

They spent the rest of the afternoon and most of the night working their way, first through midtown, then up to Harlem and down to Tribeca, avoiding Chinatown, where Uncle Chen might have eyes out for Joe. They visited bars, pool halls, backroom dice games, a couple of storefront weed peddlers, fences who specialized in art or other rare items, pizza joints, kosher delis, a fried chicken place, a Cuban-Chinese place, a regular Cuban place, and a twenty-four-hour doughnut shop. They bought rounds of drinks, lost on purpose at pool, ordered plates of food that they barely touched, and fed folded bills to waiters and bartenders and a whole bent ecosystem.

Clarence was known as a longtime heister, specializing mostly in hijacking and commercial burglaries. A bartender at a construction workers' bar that sold swag out of the back said Clarence had a cover as a real contractor, hanging drywall in Jersey, but the only evidence of it he'd seen was a truck with Jersey plates. He even found an old number, in a Rolodex, for Christ's sake, but when Joe pointed out that the number was in the 212 area code—Manhattan, not Jersey—he just shrugged. The door guy at a downtown massage parlor catering to finance guys told Joe, who told him he was checking Clarence out before taking a job, that his cousin had done time with him upstate, where Clarence was locked up for armed robbery, and that he was a stand-up guy who could be trusted. The cousin, unfortunately, was back in prison and couldn't comment. A waitress at a steak house told them that her ex-boyfriend knew Clarence and had brought him there to eat sometimes. He tipped okay and was nice, though the ex-boyfriend—a pickpocket, pool hustler, and degenerate gambler and alcoholic who liked to hit girls when drunk—was not. For fifty bucks, she told them where he hung out, at a dive bar near Union Square, hustling NYU boys. For a hundred, and a subtle threat of demasculation from Yelena, who would have been glad to even things up for his ex, the bad boyfriend coughed up the location of an apartment in the East Thirties where Clarence hosted all-night poker games. They walked by. It was a standard four-story walkup, but there was no way to tell which apartment was his—the ex-boyfriend couldn't recall an apartment or floor number, and no one had known a last name. So they cabbed it back to the hotel.

"I think maybe we should just hang out here tonight," Joe said when they got into the room. "Order room service or whatever. We put in a lot of face time today."

Yelena looked puzzled. "You need to FaceTime?" She held out her phone.

"Thanks. But I just mean we should keep a low profile and then find Clarence tomorrow."

She shrugged and kicked off her shoes. "Okay, so what do we do? I mean, before you fall asleep and start snoring like a dragon."

He pulled off his own shoes and grabbed his book before hopping onto the bed, back against the headboard. "I don't know about you, but I'm going to read."

She snorted and put her phone away. She picked up the remote and sat on the edge of the bed, zooming through the channel choices, looking back at him every few minutes. Then, with a yelp of surprise, she spoke to him in Russian.

"What?" he said.

"You are reading a Russian book. *Idiot*."

"Yes. Dostoyevsky."

"You are liking?"

"I am. I love all his books." He laid it facedown on the night table. "Actually, you have a little Filippovna in you, I think. I could see a man ruining himself for you as you throw his hundred thousand rubles in the fire."

"Ha! You must be a little bit Prince Myshkin then, an idiot. I'd never throw money in a fire. Not even rubles. They are good for toilet paper at least. My favorite is *Demons*. You know this one?"

"Yes. Why is it your favorite?"

"When I read this book I thought, *At last someone understands*." She laughed.

He leaned forward and peered at her closely. "That's a bit chilling. Because you felt like Stavrogin? I'm not sure I feel safe snoring here while you're beyond good and evil in a godless world."

She grinned and punched his arm. "No. I am not nihilist like him. Life is not meaningless. And I don't hurt the innocent. I have my beliefs. But they are not in God or man."

"I'm surprised," Joe said.

"Why?"

He touched her between her shoulder blades, lightly, in the place where the Madonna's halo rose between the straps of her dress. "This," he said.

"Oh. Ha. That is not what it means. You read Russian books but not Russian tattoos."

"Teach me."

She smiled and, turning her back to him, lowered the dress, letting it fall around her waist. "For us, religious images, like church or Mary, are good luck symbols for thieves. And the Madonna with baby means I am a child of thievery. Born into crime."

"And this," Joe asked, touching the shaded dollar sign on her left hip.

"Means I am a safecracker, as you know."

"And this?" He touched the skull, which grinned, empty eyed, from where her right hip jutted above the dress's blue folds.

"Everyone knows what a skull means," she said, still facing away from him.

"Death," he said.

"Yes, but not mine."

"It means you have killed."

She turned and faced him now, letting the dress fall away, looking him in the eye, her mouth close to his. "Any more questions?"

He laid his hands over her shoulders, where the two stars were inked. "Just these."

"Stars?" She shrugged. "Same as they mean here. They are like my badge." She smiled. "They show my high rank."

"You are royalty then," he said, kissing her mouth very softly.

"Yes," she said, holding his bottom lip between her teeth for a moment, then releasing it. "I am a princess of thieves."

34

"I ordered from the Lebanese place on Eighth Avenue."

Adrian looked up from the newspaper as Heather walked into the living room and sat on the couch beside him.

"I got enough for him, too." She waved dismissively at the guest bedroom, where Clarence had retreated to watch sports and stay out of the way.

"You mean the Israeli place?" Adrian asked.

"I think they're Lebanese," Heather said. "They have that salad I like with the beans."

"Did you go in? Hear them talking? I bet they're Jews."

"I ordered online. But actually, I think they're Egyptian. I just remembered there's a camel on the window."

"Please. Like every place with a cactus is really Mexican."

"Fine. I'll cancel. I just wanted lamb kebabs. Jesus."

"I don't care. Hummus is hummus. I'm sick of it." Adrian threw the paper down as if it were filled with articles on hummus. "What is it with white people? Hummus. Salsa. A whole culture and cuisine and you fixate on this one basic item and beat it to death. And then deport the people who make it. It's fetishistic. Like white America consuming countless tons of hummus and salsa, compulsively scooping it up with chips during every football game, every Fourth of July, obsessed with the symbol while totally denying and dehumanizing what it's a symbol of."

"You should write a term paper on it," Heather said, slumping back.

"Very funny. I'm just saying. It bugs me in a way you don't understand."

"Being fetishized as a symbol and yet dismissed as a person? No, as a blond girl I wouldn't."

"Okay. Good point . . ."

"And who are you kidding? You're from Michigan. You hate hummus, and salsa gives you heartburn."

"Okay, point taken, I said." He took her hand. "I'm sorry. I'm tense."

She pouted, pulling away.

"Honey? Are you tense, too?" He reached up under her arm and tickled.

"Stop . . ."

He grabbed her again, under the pits, and she giggled. "Please?" he said, laughing now, too. "We'll eat the Jew lamb."

She laughed and turned to him. "Shut up. You're so silly." Then she hugged him and squeezed the knot at the root of his neck. He flinched. "But you really are too tense. It's work. It's getting to you. Everything is going to work out, I promise."

"How can you be so sure?"

"Because I believe in you."

She looked into his eyes and he believed her, at least. Believed that she believed. Which was close enough. The door buzzed. She jumped up.

"That's the hummus! Go set the table."

She went to the door. He got out plates, forks, and knives. Serving spoons for the damn hummus. She came back with the bag in her hand and he had to admit it smelled good. He was starving. That was half of his anger right there, he knew.

"Fuck," she said.

"What?"

"I can't fucking believe this."

"What?"

"They forgot the lamb."

"Are you joking? Where is the delivery guy?"

"He's gone."

"I'll tell him."

"He's gone. It's just some kid."

"I'll catch him!" Adrian called over his shoulder as he ran out the door. He caught the kid at the elevator. He was a slouchy white kid with long black hair under a ball cap and a Gorgoroth T-shirt.

"Hey, you the guy who just delivered my food?"

"Yeah?"

"You brought us the wrong order. Our food is missing. There's supposed to be lamb."

"Sorry, dude, I just deliver it. I don't know what's in there."

"Well, you should take it back and bring the food we paid for."

The elevator came. The kid got on. "Can't, man. They just pay me to bring it. You got to complain to them."

Adrian got on with him. "You know what, you're right. I will."

The kid shrugged. "Whatever. I'm not even supposed to be working tonight. I missed band practice for this."

They rode in silence. "What kind of band?" Adrian asked.

"Metal. Kind of a cross between death metal and speed metal."

"Nice."

Silence returned. The doors opened. The kid looked at Adrian, a bit hesitantly. "I've got to get my bike."

"Right. I'll see you there."

The kid rolled his eyes. "Fine," he muttered, as Adrian held the door for him. The kid went to a nearby pole with a parking sign and unhooked his bike. He slid his headphones over his hat and hopped on, glancing back once more as he rose on the pedals, then pushed down and rolled into the traffic.

Adrian walked the three crosstown blocks quickly, breathing in the night air, trying to relax on the exhale the way the yoga podcasts Heather played said to. He smelled pizza as he reached Eighth Avenue and his stomach growled. Then he saw the place: Star of Sahara. With a camel and a pyramid on the window. So maybe it was Egyptian after all. He peeked into the alley next door and saw the kid's bike, locked to a pipe with a couple of others. The kitchen door was propped open and he could hear pots and pans clanging inside. Now he smelled roasted lamb. He leaned against the wall and waited a couple of minutes, thinking how maybe listening to some metal for a change might relax him more than yoga. Then the kid came back out, headphones on, a new batch of orders dangling from his arms in plastic bags. Adrian stepped into the light, his right hand held close to his side.

"Hey," the kid said, confused and too loud, deafened by the music in his head. "You've got to go in front, dude." Then, as he turned and knelt on one knee by his bike, Adrian struck. He came from behind, left hand yanking the kid's hair back—the hat and earphones slipping away, frantic machine music pouring out into the alley—as his right hand drew the razor-sharp blade across his throat. The blood gushed all over the bagged orders on the ground, splattering the white plastic, and Adrian pushed him forward, to avoid the spray. He wiped the blade quickly on the kid's jeans and went, folding it away.

Fresh lamb, he thought as he crossed the street, pulling out his phone. "Hey, honey? I've got an idea. How about pizza?"

Adrian Kaan had been born in America, but his parents were Israeli and Palestinian. A journalist and a human rights lawyer, they were peace activists, and even after they emigrated, settling in Michigan of all places, where his mother got a teaching job, they continued to visit the Middle East frequently. It was on one of these trips that their car was destroyed, caught in a cross fire between militants and Israeli fighters. Both his parents died in the front seat. Four-year-old Adrian, strapped into his car seat in back, survived.

In the aftermath, the two sides blamed each other and the incident was never resolved, but Adrian couldn't care less. He blamed both. And then, as he grew up in foster care and went on to excel in school, in sports, in hunting, in everything an all-American boy should excel in, he began to blame his new homeland. As he learned more about history, he saw how the United States continually interfered in the Middle East, at best blundering stupidly, at worst pursuing its own immediate interests with no regard whatsoever for the lives of anyone else: arming and training Afghani fighters against the USSR, the same fighters who became the Taliban, and, via the CIA, helping connect them to the opium and hash trade; supporting the shah's brutal dictatorship, thereby helping the Iranian revolution and the rule of Khomeini, leading to the hostage crisis and the Iran-Iraq War, during which the United States of course supported Saddam Hussein; and backing hard-line Israelis and West Bank settlers because that won votes at home. And the whole time patting itself on the back for being so good. And so innocent. That was the most shocking thing about the September 11 attacks: the shock itself, the disbelieving amazement that anyone in the world could want to hurt such great folks.

So Adrian trained himself, mind and body, winning a scholarship to military school, then studying history in college, where he competed in track and martial arts. Then he went overseas. He found his way into the world of the terrorists, joined their camps, underwent their training, proved himself by eventually finding the Mossad operative who had been leading the Israeli patrol that night his parents died, now retired and running a café in Tel Aviv, and slitting his throat. Not that he had anything against the Israelis in particular; at least they stood for their beliefs openly and did not pretend to be good or bad. And yes, though he went on to carry out numerous missions for the jihadists and the Palestinian freedom fighters, he also, when he learned enough to figure out who had been leading the faction of

Hezbollah that co-killed his parents, tracked that man down and killed him, too.

Then he returned to America, with his American wife, who had never really fitted in among the believers, and trimmed his beard and put on his well-made designer clothes again. And he started planning his own personal war.

35

Joe woke up when the sun through the window hit his eyes. Naked, he went to the bathroom and back. Yelena was curled in a ball, her face small and childlike as it poked from the bundle of covers. He ordered coffee from room service, and then he dialed for an outside line and called the 212 number that the bartender had given him. A number that old had to be a landline, if it was even still good. It was. Voice mail picked up, but the voice was right: "Hello, this is Clarence Deyer of Deyer Contracting. Please leave a message."

As he hung up he saw Yelena open her eyes. He smiled and squeezed her hand.

"Good morning."

She smiled back. "Good morning to you."

"I ordered coffee," he said. "And I got a last name for Clarence."

She sat up immediately. "Good," she said as she moved naked toward the bathroom. "Let's go."

* * *

Joe put on his suit and tie and Yelena her new black-and-silver leggings under a very thin, very expensive black T-shirt over a black-and-ivory lace bra. They took the train to the apartment building they hoped was Clarence's and looked over the buzzers. There it was, DEYER, 3C. Joe buzzed, just for the hell of it, but there was no response. Next they walked to a place on the corner, a small pretentious bistro. They chose a table by the window and ordered food. Neither of them spoke, except to the waitress, unless it related to the matter at hand. They were working. They ate, had coffee, took turns visiting the restroom, and saw no sign of Clarence or anyone else watching the place. They could not be sure about the other people who entered or left the building, but they doubted there was any connection: an old lady walking her poodle, a young woman with a stroller, the mailman. So they paid and went back. This time Joe easily loided the front door lock with his Irish credit card, and when they found 3C, in the back on the right, Yelena took out her picks and went through the deadbolt about as fast as most people would use a key. Guns out, they entered, Joe checking the small kitchen and bathroom, while she went through to the bedroom in back. No one. The place was empty and seemed as if it had been for some time. There was nothing in the refrigerator but condiments, and a bunch of takeout menus and coupons had been shoved under the door. The profile fit: indifferently but comfortably furnished with a saggy couch, a La-Z-Boy, a coffee table heaped with mostly sports sections and TV listings, a nice big wall-mounted flat-screen, a table in the dining area with a carousel full of poker chips in the center. It looked like the bachelor pad/gambling den of a midlevel criminal.

They started searching for anything that might lead them to Clarence or tell them who the client for the heist had been. There wasn't much. Joe did find some crumpled correspondence related to Deyer Contracting, showing an address in Lodi, New Jersey, but there was a good chance that this was nothing, too, a mail drop or an empty room. Yelena came out of the bedroom complaining about the dust and the crappy porn collection under the bed—"old DVDs of girls with each other in terrible, cheap underwear"—and when she went to the kitchen to wash her hands, the water from the faucet was brown with rust. But while she was waiting for it to clear, she happened to look through a layer of junk magnetted to the fridge. She came out smiling and handed Joe a card:

DJ Juno

SPINNING • SCRATCHING • PRODUCING • RAPPING

BEATS BUILT TO SUIT

It had a phone number, e-mail, and mailing address in Brooklyn.

"Great. Let's go," Joe said, pocketing the card. They left, quietly shutting the door behind them, and were just heading downstairs when they saw the law coming up.

36

It was tedious as hell, but Donna had to admit it was a change. Sunday had been chaos and an alphabet soup of federal, local, and state agencies stumbling all over one another at the hush-hush Westchester crime scene until the five-way pissing contest ended with the NSA and Homeland Security kicking everyone else out. Meanwhile the suspects, whoever they were and whatever they took, had gotten away clean. By Monday she was back at the office, but in another section, flipping through endless mug shots and video grabs, looking for the guy she'd briefly arrested during the arms heist. They'd narrowed the search, based on the detailed description she'd provided and the sketch their artist had produced, but the facial recognition software still showed her hundreds of men. Then, just after she'd finished a tuna salad and iced coffee, she found him. He'd done time, so he was in the system with all the trimmings: Clarence Deyer, with a last known address in Murray Hill.

She picked up the phone and called her bosses, then geared up, and by the time she got down to the garage to head out, the spooks were there. It was going to be a joint FBI and

CIA operation, with the CIA just observing, since of course they'd never operate on US soil. And the main observer? Her ex-husband, Agent Powell.

"So tell me, why does the CIA suddenly give a shit about this?" she asked as they got in the car.

"You know I can't tell you."

Donna was driving. She'd insisted, since it was US soil, and Powell was beside her, and perhaps sensing the vibe, no one else had wanted to ride with them; they all preferred to load into the van and another car.

"And you know that you'll tell me, sooner or later," she told him. "And that I can always tell when you're lying."

"Okay, just watch that truck, sheesh . . ." He winced. "We found a burned-out van in the Bronx."

"Is that news? Have you ever been to the Bronx? Was there evidence?"

"Not much, which is part of what made us curious. These guys were thorough and whoever blew it up used plastic explosives. Not the kind of thing you do after holding up a liquor store."

"Pros."

"For sure, maybe mercenaries or ex-military."

Donna thought of Joe. "And?" she asked. "So?"

"So we had our own forensics team go through it inch by inch. Or millimeter by millimeter. And what they found was a tiny charred bit of coated metal, probably from a drone."

"A drone?"

"Whatever, the point is this coated metal is used in high-tech military hardware, top-shelf stuff, just like one of the stolen items taken in your gun show fiasco."

"I get it," Donna said.

"That would also help explain how they got past the security at the lab," Mike added. "Very sophisticated business. And your pal Deyer is our first real lead."

When Donna reached the block where Clarence Deyer lived, she found the street already sealed off by an FBI car. The team was filing out of the van, in vests and FBI jackets. She pulled hers on, checked her gun, and tossed a ball cap marked FBI to Powell. "Here, put this on so you don't get shot."

"How thoughtful," he said.

"I'm only thinking of our daughter."

Since this was considered to be a personal beef for Donna, she was first through the door. She was moving quickly up the staircase, rounding floor two and heading for three, when she glanced up and saw Joe, of all people, looking over the banister at her, with some blond chick beside him.

"Hold it—FBI," she yelled, aiming her gun, but they had vanished. She called for help over her earpiece, while rushing to the door of 3C and kicking it in as Mike covered her. They cleared and secured the place, as they were trained to do—it was a real dump—but as soon as she saw the open window, Donna knew they were gone.

"Suspects have fled via the fire escape," she called. "Cover the fire escape." Then she climbed out after them.

However, Joe and Yelena did not go down the fire escape; they went up, which is why, when Donna climbed out, she just missed seeing them as they scrambled onto the roof.

As she climbed down, they crossed onto the neighboring rooftops, covering as many as they could before an alleyway stopped them. Then they went down that fire escape, hoping that they'd gone far enough to outflank the FBI.

Yelena dropped first—she was the gymnast, after all—sliding the ladder down with her, and she covered the alley while Joe climbed down. They peeked out carefully. Then, concealing their guns, they began walking arm in arm, pretending to chat and chuckle mildly, like a well-dressed couple strolling down the block and minding their own business.

They could see one FBI car parked at the corner, with a lone agent, a young black guy in a blue suit with a wire in his ear, standing guard, but watching the other way, for cars that might be coming down the street. Joe turned his head casually to the other side as they passed him, and Yelena chattered away, and they had pretty much made it, and were just waiting for a white BMW to go by so that they could cross the street, when they heard the agent yelling behind them.

"Stop! FBI! Hands in the air!"

Joe was just trying to decide what to do, moving his hands up and thinking about running, when someone in the white BMW opened fire.

Agent Newton was annoyed. As an openly gay African American agent (did he have a choice, married to Ari?), he was praised and coddled, then shunted off to secondary tasks, like guarding the corner while everyone else stormed the building. Donna Zamora was one of his main commiseration pals, though this time she was leading the charge, and he felt even more left out. Maybe he should quit and go to law school, like Ari and his mom and Ari's mom all said.

Anyway, that's what he was thinking about when he heard Donna's voice, fast over the radio: "Suspects in flight. Repeat, in pursuit. One Caucasian male, black suit, dark hair, blue eyes. One Caucasian female, also in dark clothes, blond hair." And as he heard the chatter, he realized that the well-dressed couple who had just passed by matched the description. He spun around, drawing his weapon, and there they were, the man in a suit and the woman in chic leggings and a top, waiting calmly arm in arm to cross the street. He took his stance and yelled, "Stop! FBI! Hands in the air!" And just then some Asian kid in the back of a white BMW started shooting.

When the kid opened fire, Joe and Yelena reacted, diving to the ground, Joe yelling, "Take cover!" over his shoulder at the Fed. The agent ducked behind his car. Bullets streaked its side. The agent shot back, getting off a couple of rounds as the car pulled away, while Joe and Yelena rolled out of range and ran. Turning the corner, they saw a lady climbing from the back of a cab and Yelena hopped inside.

"Where to?" the cabbie asked her.

"Just drive," Joe said climbing into the front beside him and pointing the gun at his head, while Yelena kept watch out the back.

"Holy shit, holy shit, don't kill me," the driver said, but he did as he was told and proceeded across the avenue and along the next block.

DAVID GORDON

"Don't worry," Joe said calmly. "Turn downtown." In fact he had his safety on to guard against an accidental discharge. "Now pull over here," he told him.

"Are you getting out?" the driver asked hopefully.

"No," Joe said, "you are," and hit him on the head with the gun. Then he got out and quickly, but gently, pulled the driver into the street. He got behind the wheel and pulled away, shaking off his jacket and putting on a Mets cap that the driver had left on the seat, while Yelena stayed in the back. Now they looked like a woman taking a taxi, not a couple on the run. Yelena kept her gun in her lap as Joe cruised downtown and then across Fourteenth Street.

"Who the hell was that anyway, shooting at us?" she asked.

"I think it was the Chinese Triad shooting at me, actually," Joe said. "Sorry."

Yelena shrugged. "It all worked out for the best."

186

37

Later, during the debriefing, when they were making out their incident reports, Andrew Newton told Donna a funny detail.

"Just as that kid was starting to shoot—looked like an Uzi—but anyway, the male suspect, dark hair and suit . . ."

"Right," she said. "I know the one," thinking that was Joe, but who was the girl?

"As he went down, he yelled, 'Take cover!' I could swear he was trying to warn me. Isn't that weird? Why would an armed suspect on the run care if I got shot?"

"You're right," Donna said. "That is weird."

"So, what do you think?" Andy asked her. "Should I put that in my report?"

"Probably not," she told him.

They needed to change their clothing, and didn't want to go back to the hotel, so Yelena directed them to SoHo. Joe left the cab next to a hydrant and tucked a hundred-dollar bill into the Mets cap, which he left on the seat. Once again they shopped, this time ditching their Irish identities, which they had to assume were burned, and using their other fake IDs, pretending to be a couple from L.A. Joe bought a dark blue suit, two identical white button-downs, black jeans, T-shirts, boxers, socks. Yelena bought several complete outfits and some thigh-high boots, and was trying out fragrances when he rejoined her.

"This is fun," she said, as he signed his new fake name to the charge slip.

"Remind me not to marry you for real," he told her, carrying their bags away.

"You wish," she said.

This time they hailed a taxi without hi-jacking it, and took it to a big hotel in the West Forties, a busy tourist area, trading a view for a quiet rear room.

"I hope you enjoy your stay, Mr. MacCracken," the receptionist told Joe as he charged the card.

"Please," Joe said. "Call me Phil."

While the FBI handled the crime scene forensics, Agent Powell checked the phone. He called in and had his office search the number, and sure enough, though the old, dust-covered landline had barely been used in months, it had that very morning received one call, which had gone to voice mail. The caller had left no message.

"Let's go," he said to his ex-wife when he got downstairs. "You can drive."

"Where?"

"A hotel downtown. Someone called Deyer from a room this morning."

They got in and Donna joined the sluggish flow of cross-town traffic. "Any luck ID'ing these two suspects?" Powell asked her.

"Not so far." She glanced over at him. "What? No way am I wasting another day with the sketch artist and mug shots. I barely got a glimpse. Do you think I should take Broadway?"

"Run the siren. I would if we had them."

She did, just popping it on and off to clear the lane and to keep him quiet. Why hadn't she told him about Joe? Was she instinctively protecting Joe or opposing Mike? Or was she just FBI instinctively opposing CIA? There were just too many factors she needed to understand before she risked turning this case over to the spooks, who she knew very well would never give it back. Like why, if Joe and this blond chick were Deyer's accomplices, had they picked the lock on the door, as her team had found from magnifying the tiny scratches? And what did this have to do with the lab robbery? And last, and most naggingly, she had no doubt whatsoever that if she'd caught Joe she'd have busted him, but knowing that he had almost certainly spared her and Agent Newton, too, could she have shot him down?

They got to the hotel. The girl at the front desk seemed a little rattled by the badges and by Mike looming over her, but she remembered the couple in that room.

"They're here on their honeymoon from Ireland. Isn't that sweet?"

"Ireland?" Mike asked with a frown. Were the Irish going to be mixed up in this, too? A lot of ex-IRA had gone freelance in recent years. "Can we see the record?"

"Sure." She clicked her nails across the keys. "Here it is." She turned the screen toward Donna and Mike, who peered into it. "He said it's Gaelic," she explained. "The *g* is silent!"

Mike sounded out the name: "Mr. and Mrs. Eulich Maghanus."

Donna cracked up, while the clerk looked at them in confusion.

"Very fucking funny," Mike muttered. "What kind of fugitive makes jokes?"

Donna shrugged, but she was pretty sure she knew.

38

At first, when she found the lipstick on Gio's collar, Carol was pissed at herself. Of course. What did she think, she would escape the cliché? Did she really believe he'd be the only gangster who *didn't* have a mistress? And as a psychologist, she knew the stats, the proportion of married men who sooner or later cheated, the even higher likelihood among executives and those in roles of authority, but the fact was that Gio never did seem like the type. He still didn't. From the beginning, he'd clearly craved a real partnership, real intimacy, and trust, not for ethical reasons—his family owned whorehouses and strip clubs, after all—but as an escape from that family and that world. Gio was thrilled to find someone he could actually talk to about his feelings—his fears, hopes, dreams, regrets—something he admitted he had never done even once before in his life—someone who wanted to really share a life, an equal, and he would often brag about how his wife, the doctor, was so much smarter than he was. Carol knew better than anyone else how laser sharp Gio's brain really was behind those near-black Sicilian eyes, how sharp it had to be, for him to be who he was, but she understood. He adored their children, and she had no doubt about how much he loved her. Yes, their sex life had tapered off a bit in recent years, but they still fucked more than most couples—according to the married women she knew—and even at its most intense, the secret of their sexual connection, the thing that first fused them together, was based on raw emotion and a profound need for intimacy that they shared. That's why, even as a shrink, objectively speaking, she didn't see her husband as the type to want to bang a stripper or keep a bimbo on the side.

But then again, maybe she was just in denial. That was certainly part of their life, too. In college, of course, he'd been very discreet, vaguely talking about the restaurant his family owned, the trucks selling ices in the summer, a humble working-class clan made good. But as soon as they got serious, he got honest, outlining his family history while also explaining earnestly that his role was to help the family past all that, to bring them into the modern world. And he'd meant it. His mother, her mother, his uncle with Alzheimer's, his aunt in Florida, their kids' college funds: it was all financed by the stock portfolios and real estate holding corporations that Gio had set up and that were 100 percent legit. As for the rest? She supposed she just put it out of her mind. And didn't some part of her like it, after all, knowing/not-knowing how strong he was, a dangerous man whom people feared and respected and obeyed, but who was vulnerable with her and listened to her, when he didn't have to listen to anybody? And anyway, what about those other rich families founded by powerful and ruthless men, like the Rockefellers and Vanderbilts and Kennedys? How many dead bodies were buried under those respectable foundations? Now who was in denial?

But here was something she couldn't deny. It didn't have to mean anything, but it could mean something, or it could be nothing. Late Sunday night, coming home after the gym, trying not to wake her, he'd left his clothes in a pile by the bathroom door before getting in the shower. And in the morning, after he'd left to take the kids to school, she'd picked up his stuff and there it was, a smear of lipstick in a shade that neither she nor his mother wore.

When they got out of the subway station in Brooklyn, Joe and Yelena found a car service and took a black town car to Juno's address in Bed-Stuy, wanting to appear as legit as possible. It was a row house, a nice brick building with flowers in the window boxes behind the bars. They knocked, and almost immediately, the door was opened by a tall black man in his late twenties, wearing jeans and a wifebeater. With his shaved head, neat goatee, and hard muscles, he looked like an older, tougher, less nerdy version of Juno.

"Good afternoon," Joe said. "Is Juno here?"

The man looked them over—a white couple, the guy in a suit and the woman in what looked like a couple of grand worth of black jeans, boots, and blouse.

"Who wants to know?"

Joe smiled. So did Yelena. "Sorry," he said, "I'm Philip. This is my wife, Devorah."

"Hi," Yelena said.

"Hi," the guy said.

"We're music producers," Joe continued. "We just got in from L.A. and we want to talk to Juno about business."

"Business?" the guy asked.

"Yeah, you know, deejaying and . . ." Joe searched his memory.

"Beats," Yelena put in with a smile.

"Yeah, we love his beats," Joe added.

"All right, cool," the guy said with a grin. "You better come in then. I'm Juno's brother, Eric."

He stepped aside to let them in, and as he shut the door behind them, Joe and Yelena stepped into a comfortable living room where a very large man in a Knicks jersey and long shorts sat taking up half the couch and playing a video game with a thinner guy in jeans and a backward ball cap.

"Hey," Joe heard Eric call out from behind, "these two are looking for Juno. They want to buy his beats." Then he sensed sudden movement, and seeing the expression on the men's faces change, Joe went for his gun. He whipped around to see Eric pointing a revolver at him, while Yelena pointed her own gun at the big guy, who held a gun on Joe, while the thinner dude in the ball cap pointed his pistol at her. It was a standoff.

"Easy," Joe said. "Let's not all do something stupid."

"Y'all already did," Eric told him over his gun barrel. "In his whole life, no one ever walked in here and wanted to buy beats off my little brother."

Ball Cap spoke. "I don't think he ever even had a paying DJ gig. He just started."

"So you see," Eric said, "I know you two are full of shit. So why don't you tell me why you're really here." His eyes narrowed at Joe, who returned his gaze calmly. "White dude in a suit, I'd usually say detective. But I definitely don't get a cop vibe off of you."

"Nor hip-hop producer neither," Ball Cap put in.

Joe smiled, but his gaze never moved from Eric, who nodded his head toward Yelena. "And her . . . I don't know what to think."

Yelena sneered, gun still on the big man, who remained impassive, a mountain on the couch. "One way to find out," she told him.

"All right now," Joe said. "We're all taking it easy, remember, Devorah?" He told Eric: "You want the truth? We were on a crew that pulled a job with your brother. Things went wrong. Now we're looking for our partners and the law is looking for us."

"You saying my brother double-crossed you?"

"Nope. I'm saying someone did."

Eric's eyes shifted to the others. The kid in the hat shrugged. "Checks," he said. The big man gave a barely perceptible nod.

"Juno's been missing," Eric told them. "I got a text from him late Saturday night, just said 911. Then nothing. If I call it goes to voice mail. But Charles over there is a whiz kid like Juno."

The kid smiled modestly. "No one's like Juno, but yeah, I did some digging. And Juno switched his GPS on."

"So you can't call him," Yelena said. "But you can track him."

"Exactly, Devorah. And we were just fixing to do that when you showed up on our stoop," Eric said. "But what you say now fits with what we're thinking. Whoever's got your loot, got my brother."

"Eric," Joe said, "I believe we'd very much like to come along for this ride."

"I'm thinking that, too, Philip. But you're going to ride in the back, without guns."

Joe looked over at Yelena, who answered just with her eyes, but Joe knew what she was thinking. Even if they prevailed and got out of a shoot-out alive, they'd be no closer to Juno. He nodded.

"All right," Yelena said. "It's a deal." Then very carefully, she eased off the grip of her gun, so it hung from just a finger through the trigger guard. Joe did the same, and young Charles took them. "Thanks," he said politely to Yelena.

"You're welcome."

"Okay then," Eric said, lowering his weapon. "Now let's go get my baby brother before our mother finds out what's going on."

Juno was not having fun hanging with Don. He supposed he was a prisoner, but it was more like being a houseguest trapped with a really boring, grouchy, and potentially violent relative, something with which he had some familiarity. Don was like a white version of his mother's uncle, Willy, watching daytime TV, cursing and mumbling about how he was going to show them after all this time, eating junk food out of a greasy bag, and openly farting, like right in mid-conversation, before falling asleep on the couch. But Willy drank and Don was jacked on steroids. Big difference. Don was also running on his own ego, anger, and greed, a dangerous combo, Juno knew: if he'd decided a two-way split was better than five, then why not take it all? And why not chop off the loose end, meaning Juno?

So while Don was being decent enough, giving him the bedroom in the crappy "corporate" suite he'd rented, with his own cable TV and regular meals ordered up from nearby takeouts, Juno also understood why big bad Don was sleeping on the couch between him and the door, why he had the key cards, and why he had unplugged the phone as well as seized Juno's cell. Juno's one move had been switching on his GPS and shooting his brother that SOS text, but his brother was seriously digitally challenged, and Juno didn't know if he'd be able to follow that trail of bread crumbs. So he sat and waited for Don to set up the switch and meanwhile did his time. This was white-collar jail, but it was still jail. And it wouldn't kill Don to order some salad once in a while, or even a juice, but whatever. All Juno cared about now was getting back to Brooklyn alive.

Clarence had never been so happy to get a call as he was when Don rang. He'd spent the last twenty-four-plus hours with Adrian and Heather, and the tension was about to break him. On the surface everything was fine—Heather used the building's gym, Adrian read, they did some shopping and walked the High Line—but it was exactly that smooth surface, like a silk scarf pulled so tight it was choking, that made him conscious, with each passing minute, that the clock was ticking, and if they didn't get their hands on the vial, and on the thieves who stole it, they would take it out on Clarence and do to him what they did to that poor, dumb son-of-a-bitch Norris.

So when his phone went off Monday morning and it was Don, calling from a blocked number to set up an exchange— the vial for the cash, the whole million, that afternoon at the top of the steps in the center of Prospect Park—Clarence was utterly relieved and happily reported the news to Adrian, who was doing a crossword, and Heather, who was painting her nails and answering the clues he read out. But Clarence's relief turned back into tension when Adrian, with a smile, told him their plan. Instead of showing up alone and with a bag of cash as promised, Clarence would be going armed with a bag full of newspapers and charged with killing Don and Juno and coming back with the vial.

"I understand you want to eliminate these guys," Clarence said, while Adrian was busy shredding the newspaper, including the completed crossword, and stuffing it into a duffel bag. "And believe me it will be a pleasure to kill the fuckers after the trouble they caused me, but he set up a face-off. How can I be sure to get the drop on him?"

Adrian laughed and gave him that creepy cold-eyed smile. "You didn't think I'd trust you to go alone, did you? I will arrange for a couple of my friends to join you. You know the saying, strangers you haven't met, or something like that."

"I think it's the other way," Clarence said. "A stranger is a friend you haven't met yet."

"Exactly. Unless you try to fuck me again, and then they kill you."

Heather laughed, then Adrian chuckled, and then finally Clarence grinned awkwardly and tried to laugh, too.

"Quit scaring him," she said. "You know what, honey? I'll go myself. That way Clarence will feel safer."

Adrian frowned. "Are you sure?"

"Absolutely. I'm going stir-crazy here. We can't allow your face to be seen in public too much, pretty as it is. And it's best not to involve the others yet. And anyway, I love Prospect Park."

39

When Agents Zamora and Powell got back to her office, she sat and began checking her e-mail while he stood over her desk. He cleared his throat.

"Have a seat, Mike," he said, imitating and exaggerating her slight New York accent. "Want a cup of coffee?" He moved some files from a chair and sat, switching back to his own flat midwestern voice: "Why, thank you, Donna, I'd love some."

"What's the fucking point?" Donna asked then, looking up from her screen.

"Fucking point of what?"

"People who sit around on their asses drinking coffee in an office together usually work together. But if you're going to go on pretending to be a CIA liaison helping with an FBI investigation, while not even telling me who or what we're chasing, then what, I ask, is the fucking point?"

"Like you've been totally forthcoming?"

"Hey, I'm an open book. Or an open file at least. I will let you read anything you want. Can you do the same?"

"You know I can't."

"So?"

"All right. But I could really use that coffee first."

She got the coffee and came back to see him casually flipping through a file, one she knew had nothing but transcripts of old tip-line recordings, but, still, he couldn't help himself, a compulsive snoop.

"What?" he said to her dirty look. "You said help myself."

"Not quite." She took her seat. "But whatever. It's your turn."

He sipped his coffee. "Yuck. It's better at your house." He put it down on the closed file. "Okay," he said. "Here goes. The item that was stolen from the lab was a highly effective bio-agent capable of transmitting a lethal virus over a wide range, whether through the air or through the exhalations of the infected."

"Jesus . . ." Donna's mind immediately bypassed years of training and instantly turned to her own daughter. Their daughter. Did his? "And we made this?" she asked him. "The good guys? Who? CIA? Some other pals of yours?"

"The lab was actually trying to dilute it, testing micro-doses in different solutions so that it could be used to target an individual or a group, instead of just unleashing mass destruction, which you know very well we'd never do."

"Except that you are, through incompetence maybe, but still. And why the hell wasn't something that nasty in a government facility?"

"That was a government facility. The security firm was a CIA front. The technology they used to alarm the place isn't even commercially available. The perfume company is legit, but we are the shadow partners and we designed the safe and the locking mechanism for the lab. Look"—he held his empty palms out—"it's not like it was my idea. I just found all this out after the break-in. But the thinking, as I understand it, was hide in plain sight, a regular old lab that no one would care about or notice."

"Plus," she added, "it was a black op, no doubt."

"Yes. A major fuckup. But the point now is to get it back before they can use it."

"And who is 'they'?"

"Terrorists. ISIS or someone else."

"I'm no profiler, but Clarence Deyer doesn't strike me as the jihad type."

"No. I'd say he's definitely nonideological. He's just the hired help. And the front man. The end user is a very different breed."

"Who?" Donna asked.

"Him." Mike pointed at the leftmost photo of the watch list on her wall, a disturbingly handsome blue-eyed man with buzzed hair and the scruffy cheekbones of a model. "Adrian Kaan. Number one most wanted, and here in New York right now."

"Oh." Mechanically, she sipped her cold bitter coffee, then threw it into the trash. "How can you be so sure?"

"We can't, but the evidence points that way. Chatter on ISIS and terrorist-connected forums has been all about him, how he was seen in New York."

"Forums! It's like kids blabbing about a pop star."

"He is a pop star to them. A terrorist the old whitebeards don't even approve of. He went through their training camps, then broke off and went rogue. He isn't even Muslim. He's just fucking evil. Anyway, the young jihadists think he's cool. And then this was issued, from a server in Indonesia that he's used before."

Mike pulled something up on his tablet and handed it to her.

Hello America!
When will you learn you can't outsource pain?
Globalization isn't just cheap T-shirts. It's war. And now the war you sent us is coming home to you.

Donna sighed. "I would definitely call this ideological."

"If total nihilistic destruction counts as an ideology." He sipped his cold coffee, frowned, and threw it into the trash with hers. "But there's one thing I still can't figure."

"What's that?"

"What the hell do the Chinese have to do with it?"

40

When Juno said that all he wanted was to get back to Brooklyn alive, he did not mean an armed exchange in the park with himself as the go-between, but he guessed that's what they meant about watching what you wished for. It had been a long time since he'd hung out here, but as Don, casually holding a pistol to Juno's back, marched them through the park and up the hill, climbing the concrete steps to the paved plaza that overlooked the park from the top, he flashed on all the times he'd been here as a kid, playing ball, or riding bikes, or having cookouts. He saw the bikers and softball players now, the picnickers and sunbathers scattered over the meadow, a happy Australian shepherd leaping for a ball, and swore, if he survived, to swing by and rejoin them soon. Get out and enjoy the fresh air the way his mom said, instead of sitting inside and gaming or hacking all the time. Of course, he knew he would do no such thing.

When they got to the top of the steps, Don put his hand on Juno's shoulder. "Hold it here," he said. He put the pistol in the back of his belt and shouldered the AK he'd been hiding under a jacket. Then he handed Juno the vial cased

in plastic. This was the first time Juno had actually held the thing. The million-dollar perfume, if that's what it really was. Whale sperm or not, this was starting to seem like a lot of drama over smelling good. He'd had plenty of time over the last day and night to think about what it was, and he hoped it was the cure for AIDS or cancer, but something told him this was not a bunch of humanitarians he was involved with.

Then Don spotted Clarence on the other side of the clearing, holding a duffel bag, as instructed. "Okay," Don said, prodding Juno with the barrel, "let's do this."

Heather took up her position. She had arrived early, in her running gear, with the sniper rifle dismantled in a small backpack. She jogged through the park and up the stairs toward the plaza where the meeting would take place, then took cover in the trees, lying flat in a spot where she commanded a clear view. She assembled her rifle, then lay still, while insects hummed slowly through the air around her, and birds warbled and screeched, jumping incessantly from twig to twig in the summer-green trees above. She was thinking about the vacation she and her husband would take, beginning the second this mission was over. She'd already booked the tickets, under false names, of course, and chosen a hotel. She imagined herself under a different, deeper, bluer sky, a closer sun, dozing beside him, hand at rest in his. She'd shut her eyes then, against the glare, and only the ocean would whisper into her ears.

Then she saw the young black kid arrive at the top of the stairs, with the muscle head, Don, prodding him from behind with a gun. She shifted into shooting position. When she saw Clarence arrive at the other end, holding the duffel bag full of newspaper, she pressed her eye to the scope. Ideally, he would kill or try to kill those two and she would kill him, but it didn't really matter, as long as they all died and she brought the virus home to her husband.

When Don grunted, "Let's do this," Juno held his hands out to show he had the vial and no weapon, and began, very carefully, to walk. The plan was that he'd cross over, exchange the vial for the bag of cash, and then come back, while Don covered Clarence with the AK. Of course, Juno realized that Don had no intention of sharing the money, but would he kill Juno over it or just ditch him? And how, Juno wondered, could he not find out, by escaping the fuck out of here, with or without the money? The fact that he could, in theory, just catch the bus home made the idea that he was caught in a possibly fatal trap even more of a weird nightmare.

He reached Clarence. Feeling a bit awkward, he instinctively smiled. "Hey, Clarence, sorry 'bout the mess," he said, holding out the vial.

Clarence shrugged. "It's cool, kid," he said, taking it and handing over the bag. "All in a day's work."

Then Juno heard a shot go off behind him and saw the look of panic on Clarence's face. He spun around to see Don firing wildly into the air, as his brother, Eric, of all people, grabbed him from behind. Juno turned to dodge the flying bullets, only to see Joe grabbing Clarence and yanking him back. And his own pal Charles was with him in his trademark Marlins cap. It was like a surprise party. Juno broke into a run toward Joe and Charles, away from Don's gun, when someone else, someone out in the woods, took a shot and blew up the bag in his hand. Shredded newspaper exploded like a piñata.

"Motherfucker!" he yelled, partly at Clarence for faking the cash, partly at whoever was shooting at him. The word just came out like other folks yelled "Geronimo." Then Juno took off at top speed into the trees.

When they got to the park, Charles, who was tracking Juno's phone on his own phone, led them all—Joe, Yelena, Eric, and the still silent big man—straight to the base of a large hill covered with trees and with a flight of stone steps running up the side.

"According to this, Juno must be right at the top," he told them.

"You know this spot?" Joe asked. "What's the layout like?"

"Sure," said Eric. "We've been coming here our whole life. These steps go up to, like, a paved area where you can sit on top. There's more steps going down the other side."

"If you don't mind a suggestion," Joe said, "I think you and Yelena should go up these steps, while Charles and I take the other side. That way we have a gun covering both exits."

"What about the big man?" Eric asked. The man in question also turned to Joe.

"If it's all right with you," Joe told him, "I'd say you should cut up that path through the woods there and circle around. That way you can take down anyone who slips past us."

"Sounds good," Eric said. The big man nodded and immediately took off, jogging at a surprisingly good clip; it was like seeing your refrigerator suddenly jump up and move.

"Give us a minute's head start," Joe said, and turned to Yelena. "See you at the top," he told her with a wink.

She smiled. "I will be waiting."

Joe and Charles took off running, Joe now naturally taking the lead, Charles happy to follow even though he was the one with the gun. Not to mention he was winded at the top, when Joe suddenly stopped and put a hand out, like, *Halt.* Charles halted. Then Joe crept up slowly, and peeking after him, Charles saw what Joe saw: this white guy, older, with a bald patch in the back, talking with Juno. Then shots cracked out. Juno jumped, and before Charles could do anything, Joe had snatched the white guy back from behind and was pinning him down with a knee right on his throat.

"Charles, point the gun at him," Joe said.

"Right, sorry," Charles said, and did it. He'd been a little stunned.

Joe eased his knee off the guy's throat, but when he tried to sit up, Joe pushed him back with his knee now on his chest. He held up the plastic box the guy had been holding.

"What is it?" he asked.

"Joe, listen, I'm not the one who crossed you. It was Don and the kid—"

"What is it?" Joe asked again, pressing harder against the man's solar plexus.

"It's a bug," he gasped.

"A bug?" Joe and Charles both looked at the clear plastic. To Charles it looked like the urine sample he'd had to give when he got busted for weed that one time.

"Like a virus," the guy went on. "It's germ warfare shit."

"Where's the client?" Joe asked.

"He's waiting for me to call him. Here . . ." He reached for his pocket and Charles almost shot him out of pure nervousness, but the guy yelled, "Phone! I'm just getting my phone," and slowly pulled a disposable flip phone from his pocket.

Joe took the phone and eased back, releasing the guy, who sat up, rubbing the sore spot on his abdomen, just a few inches below the spot where the wound suddenly bloomed when the bullet went through his heart.

"Jesus!" Charles yelled, as Joe called out, "Take cover," but Charles already was scampering back down the steps. Joe took off running the other way, up to the top of the hill, and was gone.

When Heather saw the exchange going wrong, she took her first open shot. It was at Juno, and she missed. Juno had, maybe accidentally, done the smart thing, running for cover in a chaotic and jagged fashion, making it much harder to aim accurately. Heather was an excellent shot, and if he'd run in a straight line she would have picked him off, no problem, instantly calculating his speed relative to that of the bullet. But, as it happened, his erratic movements threw her just slightly and saved his life. She missed him and tore through the bag full of newspaper. Before she could get another shot off he was gone, into the woods.

Heather couldn't see Don now, but swiveling left she could see Clarence through the trees, struggling with another white man she didn't know. Clarence was now a liability—he knew too much—so when the man backed off and she saw a clear target, she shot him through the heart. She was about to kill the white guy next, whoever he was, when she heard something crashing through the woods behind her, like a bear or a whole platoon. She rolled over, but the foliage in which she was so cleverly hidden made it impossible to turn around and fire quickly. She had just enough time to glimpse a huge black guy, like a football player, jumping on top of her.

He weighed a ton. Just the impact squeezed the breath out of her, almost knocking her unconscious. As it was, she was immobilized with her rifle uselessly trapped beneath her. She began squirming, looking for leverage, some small opening from which to punch him in the balls or something. But like the well-trained wrestler he was, he moved quickly to keep her effectively pinned. But this wasn't wrestling, and instead of tapping out, Heather bit him, hard, right through the ear. She tasted blood and felt him jerk away but only clamped down harder, locking her jaw.

The big man screamed, instinctively rising up as he shook loose. And that gave her a chance. She got her free arm around his neck. It was like a tree, it felt as thick as her waist, but as he grappled with her, she found the point on his vein and pressed, hard and steady, keeping the pressure on even after he realized what was happening and, in desperation, smacked her on the side of the face with his huge hand, before slipping into a deep and dreamless sleep.

It took several precious minutes for her to get out from under him. She felt as if she was buried alive. She exhaled completely, making her body even smaller, and wriggled a little bit, then again. Finally she got an arm free and grabbed on to a root. Using that as leverage, she managed, with a moan, to slither out. She got unsteadily to her feet. Her whole body ached and she could feel her face already swelling. Her rifle was still hidden somewhere beneath him, and he was beginning to mumble, slowly regaining consciousness, so she left it there and ran.

As soon as Yelena and Eric got to the top of the hill and she saw him go for Don, she knew he was making a mistake. But it was too late to say so, and he hadn't asked. Men rarely did ask. He was worried about his brother, which was understandable, and why would a muscular man, over six feet tall, ask a slender young woman who barely reached his shoulder how to fight? Plus, he had a gun.

So Eric grabbed Don by the left shoulder, with his left hand, and jabbed the pistol into his right side, causing Don to jerk his arm up and fire randomly. Eric should have grabbed him by the throat and yanked back, throwing Don off balance. Or knocked him out with the gun. Or else just shot him. But as it was, he gave Don the chance to do what she would have done. As soon as he felt the poke of what he knew was a weapon, he spun right, slashing out with his elbow and knocking Eric's gun into the woods. Then Don followed through, completing his turn, bringing his left fist up hard to clout Eric hard on the side of the head and knock him sideways, ear no doubt ringing. He then tried to bring his own weapon, the AK-47, up from his side and into play. But by then Yelena was on him.

Already moving when Don moved, knowing what would happen, she had jumped, leaping over Eric as he stumbled sideways, and kicking the rifle from Don's grip into the trees. But before she could get another blow in and finish him, Don had grabbed her in a bear hug and they went over together, struggling as they tumbled down the steps.

At the bottom she was up first, springing backward, cat-like, kicking out as he rose and clipping him on the chin. He fell back, onto the steps, and she was closing in when his hand came up holding another gun, this one a flat automatic.

"Hold it," he yelled. And she listened. She froze in motion, putting her hands up, and even stepping back, giving Don room to stand and giving Joe, whom she saw coming swiftly down the steps, a chance to jump him from behind.

Joe did not make a mistake. He grabbed Don by the neck, locking his left biceps tight around his throat, while his right arm seized Don across the forehead to grip on the base of his skull. In one smooth movement, he broke Don's neck.

Part IV

41

Charles took the big man to the ER to get his ear stitched up. They said he got bitten by a dog, which meant threatening him with rabies shots, but otherwise he was fine. Eric took the rest of them back to their place, Juno beside him in front, the two brothers' arms around each other the whole way, Yelena and Joe in the back. When they got home, he gave them their guns.

"Sorry," he said. "I see now I should have let you hold them."

"That's okay," Joe said, and shook his hand.

Yelena shrugged. "Turns out we didn't really need them," she said, and they shook hands, too.

"So then, what are you going to do with this?" he asked, pointing to the encased vial, which sat on the coffee table, atop a stack of magazines, like a weird modern paperweight.

"I'm out," Juno said, shaking his head. "I have no problem stealing some rich lady perfume. Shit's already a rip-off. But this? I say turn it over to the cops or whoever. The dudes in the hazmat suits. What about you, Joe?"

"It's been a really exciting weekend," Joe said, "but I didn't go through all this to walk away empty-handed. I say we call the client and see what he offers."

"It's all yours," Juno said. "I'm happy just to be alive."

"No," Joe said. "You put in the work. You still get your cut."

"Thanks, man. You're all right," Juno said. He asked Yelena, "What about you?"

"I'm with Joe," she said.

When Heather got home and told Adrian what happened, he saw her swollen cheek and he was furious, mainly at himself.

"I never should have let you go." He got an ice bag from the freezer. "I can't believe I put you in harm's way."

"Please. I've had worse injuries in kickboxing class and you know it." She lay back on the couch as he handed her the ice bag. "Thanks, baby." She squeezed his hand. "I'm glad you worry about me. I feel the same about you, but you know I can take care of myself."

"I know you can, better than anybody," he said, kneeling by the couch. He lifted her shirt to kiss her belly. "But now you have my son to take care of, too."

She laughed, ruffling his hair. "Your daughter doesn't even have lungs yet. Or eyes. She is just a tiny blob of cells."

"Still." He sat on the floor and leaned his head against her. "I couldn't bear to lose you both."

"You won't," she said, and stroked his head without further argument. She knew he had abandonment issues.

42

Gladys was just sitting down to watch *Jeopardy!* when Gio stopped by.

"Hi, hon," she said as he leaned down to kiss her, "help yourself in the kitchen," then hurried back to her chair.

"Oh, right, it's time for Alex," Gio said. "Sorry, I forgot."

He went into the kitchen and got a Fresca, then sat quietly on the couch and waited for the commercial. He knew better than to interrupt.

"Who is Milton?" she yelled at the screen. "Where is Zimbabwe? What is the clavicle? Clavicle, you idiot." The tension was palpable as the little buzzers *beep-beep*ed. "Radium! I mean, what is radium? Take geography for five hundred, dummy. What are the Himalayas? Himalayas!"

She sat back and took a breath, seeming to notice Gio for the first time. "Oh, good, you got a Fresca. Put a little in here for me." She held out her glass, which she'd emptied but for the ice. He poured in the Fresca and she topped it up with some whiskey. "So what's new? How's the family?"

"Good. Nora's soccer team is undefeated so far—"

"God bless. I think it's great how nowadays girls will do anything. And how's your mom?"

"Fine. The same."

"Send her my best."

"I will. And how are you?"

She waved her hand over her domain. "As you see, no complaints."

"Have you heard from Joe? I'm trying to reach him."

She sipped her drink, leaving a fresh lipstick print. "You and everybody else. But I guess he's too busy to call me."

"Who else?"

"This nice lady Fed. Spanish name . . . I've got her card somewheres." She began looking around, moving things. "Now where did I leave them?"

"The card?" Gio asked, looking over the coffee table.

"No. My glasses."

"They're on your head."

"Oh, ha . . . silly me." She reached up into her hair and pulled them out, then set them on her nose. "Okay, then, let's see . . ." Gio waited and smiled encouragingly. "Oh, here it is, right in my pocket. Sorry." She peered at it. "Donna Zamora?"

"I know Agent Zamora," Gio said.

"Cute, right? Nice little bod on her, too."

"Sure."

"I think she's sweet. For a cop." She took another sip.

"What did you tell her?"

"What do you think? Zilch."

He smiled. "And what do you think she wanted?"

"You know what I think? I think she has a little thing for Joey."

Gio laughed. "Okay, Gladys, thanks for the Fresca. And if Joe gets in touch, tell him to call me. I don't want to worry you, but it's important." He stood up and bent to kiss her.

"I'm not worried. Joe can take care of himself. And me sometimes." She pinched his cheek. "And you, too, Gio."

He grinned. "I know it."

When Gio walked out, keys in hand as he strode toward his car, already on the phone like the multitasking executive he was, Donna was watching. She'd come by a couple of hours before, just on her own, and parked discreetly up the block and sat, on the hunch that if the elusive Joe were going to pop up anywhere, it might be at Grandma Gladys's apartment, which was his only known abode, unless "back booth in a strip club" counted as an abode. Gio had turned up instead.

She considered bracing him, but what was the point? Either he was relaying a message for Joe, in which case he'd tell her squat, or more likely he was looking for him, too, in which case he knew squat, maybe less than she did. So no surprises there.

The surprise came next. She was sitting back, out of eye-shot, letting Gio's car pass by, when she realized he was being followed. As soon as Gio started his engine, another car a few spots farther along had started up. And when Gio pulled out, this one came right after, driven by a dark-haired woman. A Volvo wagon, hardly the gangster's choice. Or the cop's, for that matter. Still, she could swear it was on Gio's tail, and not very professionally. So she ran the plate and bingo: it belonged to Carol Caprisi, Gio's wife.

Now why would a crime boss's wife be tailing her own husband? Donna sighed. This whole case was a mess. She pictured her ex-husband, the CIA brain, standing in front of a whiteboard, trying to decide whether this newest red line should connect to CHINA or ISIS or even IRA. A tangled web. Or not even a web, more like a knot she'd brushed out of her daughter's hair. You tossed it into the trash. You didn't try to untangle it. And thinking of her daughter, who was eating with Donna's mom, and how soon she'd be ready to take her bath and have her hair brushed before bed, she drove home.

When Donna pulled out—already on speakerphone with her mom, to say she was on the way, keep dinner warm—she didn't notice that Agent Mike Powell was watching. He'd been trailing his ex-wife, discreetly, since their chat in her office, when he'd felt certain she was holding back something. What was less certain was why he felt that or why he thought it mattered.

He'd learned in his years spent in the nebulous world of spies and counterspies to listen to his own gut over everything. But the one problem with that was your gut sometimes malfunctioned when it came to your personal life. It seemed to go haywire and whisper crazy things that made you paranoid over nothing, or else tell you everything was fine when you and your gut were both heading straight for disaster. It had cost him, too, during his divorce, when it came out that he'd been using company resources to check up on his wife. The rebuke, though harsh, was unofficial. The company, ever mindful of appearances, could not have word get out that an agent was using it for personal reasons, nor that it was involved in anything at all on US soil, which was strictly forbidden. So nothing went in his file, but he was passed by for promotion, left behind when everyone else was getting into tastier stuff overseas. He'd crossed the line.

And now here he was, spying on his own ex-wife as she drove home to see their daughter, ostensibly following up on an investigation, on US soil, in which the CIA was passionately involved. So where was that line again?

And what did his gut tell him about this Joe Brody, who kept popping up in his case and his wife's—or rather, he corrected himself, his ex-wife's—life? He wasn't sure. Just that Brody was a threat. And one thing both he and the CIA did quite well was eliminate threats.

Carol had been following her husband around all day, and, frankly, his life was not as exciting as she had imagined. Her own routine, of seeing patients in her therapy practice and shuttling her kids around, seemed to contain more drama. Gio drove to some nondescript, often pretty dismal-looking business—an office, or bar, or warehouse—hugged or shook hands, talked, drank coffee, shook or hugged again, and went to the next spot. Repeat. Finally he drove into his old neighborhood and parked in front of a familiar building. This seemed like something more interesting, a clue perhaps, until she remembered it was where his childhood pal Joe, the one with PTSD and a dope problem, lived with his grandma. She'd been here once or twice over the years, to bring a cake or a gift. And Joe had been at their place for holidays. He was a charming, likable guy, and Gio felt sorry for him. He was surprisingly sentimental that way. Carol had suggested therapy, of course, probably individual and a support group of vets, and rehab maybe. And meds. But that fell on deaf ears. Stick him in a corner and give him a little job, like doorman at a club. Sad really, how we as a society treated our vets.

Anyway, that was that. Gio left there and actually called her from the car, which made her feel guilty so she didn't pick up. He left a voice-to-text message saying he'd had a long day and was stopping by the gym to work out, maybe spar a little. And she didn't blame him. It did seem that if she were he, she'd need some kind of release, too. So maybe, even though she was snooping, it was healthy? She was learning more empathy for her husband? Or was that just rationalizing? What would she tell a client?

She'd tell her to stop spying on her partner, to respect his privacy, and to go home. And she was about to do just that, even calling the nanny to say she was on the way, when instead of driving toward the gym, Gio pulled off the highway and led her to the parking lot of a cheap motel. At least he had his gym bag.

43

Gio called Paul from the car. He had a delivery for him, a bag of cash, tribute he'd collected on his rounds that day. Paul said he could come to the office or pick it up at Gio's house, but Gio suggested the Easy-Rest Motel instead. That way they could get a little private time in, too. Paul said he'd be happy to.

So he called his wife and was a little relieved when she didn't pick up. He found it a bit easier to lie to her phone than to her. But then why bullshit himself, too? He'd been lying in one way or another since they'd met. Still, those were lies of omission, saying a late-night call was a "business problem," and yes, it was, technically, but it went unsaid that solving the problem involved breaking somebody's legs. They collaborated on those lies; he didn't want to tell her and she didn't want to know. She understood. But this she would not understand. Even with her degrees and her "embracing difference" and whatnot. It was like two different worlds. She'd even asked him if he allowed trans persons to use the gendered restroom of their choice in his places. What was he supposed to tell her? That in his places there were men who actually paid to *be* the toilet, never mind worrying about which one to use?

That thought amused him, and he was already feeling a little less stressed, even chuckling to himself, as he pulled into the motel lot, grabbed the money bag, and went in to see his accountant.

By the time Carol was able to turn safely, find a discreet spot to park down a side street, and walk back to the Easy-Rest Motel, she had no idea where Gio had gone. It was a two-story building with rooms top and bottom, the upper ones connected with a balcony. Two smaller wings extended on either side, one containing the office and presumably the laundry and supply rooms, the other a little cocktail lounge, which according to a neon sign in the window was called EZ's. So, playing detective, and feeling both foolish and frightened, she tried walking past the ground-level row of rooms, each with a flimsy door and a window. All were dark and presumably empty, except one where kids could be seen jumping on the bed. She went up the exterior flight of steps and tried the upper floor. Here, several were lit from within, with the draperies closed, and she had to move more slowly, trying to somehow look as if she was taking a casual stroll while pressing her face to the windows and peeping. Her heart pounded; sweat crept down her armpits and scalp. She told herself she was crazy, out of control. But she kept going.

The first lit window showed a guy in a towel looking in his suitcase. She saw him only from behind, but it was not Gio. He pulled out some socks. She moved on. In the next lit room she saw a fellow mom, a bit younger than herself, African American, lecturing two small kids, who listened with intense seriousness. Behind the next door she heard arguing in Spanish. Next, a TV playing sports. She couldn't see the viewer, but she doubted Gio was here for that. On the whole it turned out that being a detective was even duller than being a gangster. Then, in the last room, she saw something interesting.

She saw a woman. And she didn't like to say this—it was only a partial view from the back, and the woman was moving, and the light was very dim—but . . . well, she was unattractive. Ungainly, with a not very graceful figure. Also she was dressed badly. She looked trashy, in a tight-fitting lace dress that had long sleeves and a kind of ruffle at the hem, over black hose and some very unfortunate red heels that didn't even look like real leather. She had long, stringy, unkempt blond hair. She looked, to be frank, like a cheap slut and a very cheap one at that, except that, as she walked, Carol caught a glimpse of a gold band, a wedding ring, flashing quickly on her hand. So she was married. She was showing herself to, or maybe trying on the tacky dress for, a man whom Carol could not make out, seated in a chair off to the side. She could see his suit pants and tried to recall what color slacks Gio was wearing. And then—and this made Carol hold her breath—the blond woman lay across the man's lap, and he lifted her dress, revealing a really atrocious pair of sparkly panties, and started spanking her, hard. And as he moved, leaning forward to smack her better, Carol caught a glimpse of the man's face. And now she did gasp and quickly ran away, in a panic, terrified that they had heard her. Because she knew him. He was Paul, her husband's accountant.

Carol was dumbfounded. This, as detectives, or rather detective novelists, would say, was a twist in the case. In a daze, she walked to her car. Then, deciding she had to think things through, she called the nanny back and begged her to stay one more hour, saying she'd run out of gas. She walked on, aimlessly, until she saw a small corner shop and went in. She bought a pack of American Spirits, smoked one, and threw the rest away. Gio hated her smoking, and she didn't let him know that she occasionally indulged when under stress, like right now. Automatically chewing her mint gum, she decided to walk back by the motel for one more quick look.

But she could see, even from the lot, that the room in question was now dark. Paul and his mystery woman, the trashy slut who needed a spanking apparently, were either gone or in bed, with the lights out. But Gio's car was still parked in a corner. She made another, slower patrol around the perimeter of the property, and when she got to the far side, she peeked into EZ's lounge. And there was Gio, sitting in a booth, nursing a beer with his gym bag beside him and staring up at the game. She lingered by the door and watched as the back door, which led to the rooms, opened and Paul came in. Gio called and waved, and Paul waved back, stopping for a beer of his own before joining him. They talked and laughed, and Gio handed over the bag.

Carol's phone buzzed. It was a text from the nanny, asking if she should make dinner, and taking that as her cue, Carol left. She'd seen enough. She understood.

When Gio got home that night, dinner was a bit late and the kids were antsy. Carol said she'd run out of gas or nearly. She'd managed, almost running on fumes, to pull into a station. Gio scolded her mildly—what if the kids had been with her?—and then checked to make sure the AAA membership had been renewed. Later, as they stood in their own room, absentmindedly disrobing, Carol asked, casually, "You know who I happened to think of today? Paul. That nice accountant. I haven't seen him in ages."

Gio looked at her sharply. "That's funny," he said. "It just so happens I saw him today, for a beer."

"Oh?"

"I had some cash to give him. You know that account he set up for me, for us?"

"Yes . . ." It was a secret account in the Cayman Islands. He'd made her write the number on a tiny scrap of paper, then hide it in the head of their daughter's old doll.

"He thinks we should split it up, move some to the Hebrides or wherever. It's like a whole world tour with these guys, but whatever . . ." He kissed her cheek. "If I disappear tomorrow, you'll be a very rich widow."

She rolled her eyes. "Don't even say that. But I'm glad you saw him. How's he doing?"

"Fine."

"Is he seeing anyone?"

Gio shrugged indifferently and took off his pants. "I guess."

"But no one special?"

Gio scowled and went into the bathroom. "How would I know? Why do you care?"

"No reason." She followed him, standing in the doorway while he put toothpaste on his brush. "I just thought maybe you'd like to invite him to dinner sometime, and if he has a partner, to invite them both. He's a nice young man."

Gio pulled the toothbrush from his mouth and waved it, splotching the mirror. "I'll invite him to the barbecue like everybody. But that's it. You know I like to keep these things separate."

She did. In fact he didn't know, or at least didn't speak, about his employees' lives at all. She learned about their children's births and their divorces secondhand. Now she felt she knew more about Paul than Gio did. She had always guessed he was gay and keeping it a secret from the macho guys in Gio's world. But now she knew the truth. She understood his secrecy, why he always showed up for parties alone, even why he had used a meeting with Gio to cover his hidden rendezvous: Paul was having an affair with an older, married woman.

44

Joe and Yelena ate dinner, ordering room service to minimize their exposure. Afterward, Yelena ran the bath and began shedding her clothes.

"Want to join?" she asked, holding up the bottle of vodka she'd been icing.

"You go ahead," Joe said. "I think I'll make some tea first."

He stood at the small countertop, which held a microwave as well as bottled water, cups, spoons, and the basket containing the other stuff the hotel left out for them, like assorted tea bags, a fancy scented candle, and some chocolates. Placed prominently in the center of the gift basket, as a joke, but also as a precaution, was the artfully designed clear plastic case, which they now knew contained not perfume, but a deadly disease. Joe reached for a cup.

"Don't use the bubble water," Yelena told him. "The tea will be gross."

"Good point. I'll be right with you," he called, as she stalked away and shut the door.

Once she was gone, he got out the last Dilaudid he'd been saving, wrapped in a bit of paper. He crushed it in a spoon and then added flat water. He lit a hotel match to dissolve it, then lit the scented candle, too, as cover. Joe got the sealed syringe he'd hidden in the lining of his jacket, loaded it, and carefully injected himself, using his tie as a tourniquet. Instantly, the knot in his stomach began to untangle, and the throbbing inside his skull lessened, as if a volume knob were dialing down. Pleasure—warm numbness, dumb darkness—threaded his veins, circulating forgetfulness and sleep. He snapped the needle, for the safety of the maid, and threw it into the trash.

"Joe, hurry! Fuck the tea!" Yelena yelled from behind the bathroom door, as he sat, soaking up his own inner warmth and meditating on the million-dollar box.

When Yelena got out of the tub, after a long hot soak and a fair amount of cold vodka, she saw Joe conked out on the bed again, still clothed, and with the tea unmade. Just a cup of water cooling in the microwave.

"Joe, Joe, you really are getting too old for me," she teased, as she brushed her wet hair and tossed the loose nest of tangled strands into the trash. It fell on the floor and, leaning to pick it up, she saw something shiny in the wastebasket. It was a used and broken syringe, wrapped in tissues. Looking closely at Joe's left arm, she found the little mark. She put the needle back into the trash and then got into bed. He mumbled and, sensing her presence, wrapped his arms around her, then drifted off again, eyelids dropping.

"I understand," she whispered to his vacant form. "It is painful to kill someone, even when it is a pleasure."

45

In the morning, Joe woke up feeling much better. Well rested, he drank a black coffee, showered, and even shaved. Then he put on his suit and tie while Yelena, dressed in jeans and a black top, finished packing. They would locker their bags at Penn Station and pick them up when, or if, they could.

"I think we've let them stew long enough," he told her. He got out Clarence's phone, went to the long list of missed calls, all from the same name and number, and hit dial.

"Hello?"

"Good morning," Joe said. "You must be Adrian."

"That's correct. And to whom do I have the pleasure of speaking?"

"Just call me Joe."

"Well, Joe, you could be a bit more imaginative in your choice of pseudonyms, but I like your simplicity. Let's hope the rest of our relationship is this straightforward. I believe you have something I want to buy?"

"I do indeed."

"And the item is in good condition?"

"Mint condition. Still in the original packaging."

"Fantastic. And the price?"

"I believe you quoted Clarence a figure of one million?"

"Right, but that was to cover five people and a lot of expenses. You're only one man. Or are you?"

"Like you said, let's keep things simple and stick with an even million."

"Fine. I'm not in the mood to quibble, and I have it ready, so when and where do we meet?"

"I'm ready anytime. Someplace nice and public."

"Do you know where the High Line is?"

"I do."

"I happen to know a building, right beside it, that has a parking garage. We can meet on level three, nice and public. Say, after lunch? At two?"

"Sounds perfect."

Adrian gave him the address, and Joe repeated it while Yelena listened. "I look forward to meeting you, Adrian," he said.

"And I you. Bye, Joe."

Adrian was adamant. Heather was not coming with him.

"It's got nothing to do with bullets, baby. Or with how tough you are. There's just no way I am—I mean *we* are— going to risk exposing the baby to this virus. Who knows what kind of damage it could do, even at the molecular level? This is the first time it's ever been used."

She gave him a kiss. "I'm going to agree," she said. "Only because you're being so cute."

It was decided that she would steal the getaway car from the long-term section of the garage in their building and then wait, idling on the street outside, to take them both to the airport when he was done.

Adrian called in the Three Stooges, who were camped out in a nearby hotel, watching pay-per-view porn. Really their names were Amar, Troy, and Mike, and they were all members of the cell Adrian had worked with in Europe, but Heather called them Larry, Curly, and Moe, because they always showed up together and because they were, in her mind, mere flunkies. But now she greeted them warmly and served coffee, while Adrian told them what they needed to know.

Meanwhile Heather prepared the money. They had nothing like a million in cash and had never planned to pay that much to anyone. They took the real cash, crisp new hundreds, and used it, top and bottom, on stacks of blank paper cut to size, then banded. They also took a large amount of counterfeit cash produced in North Korea—decent but not anything they'd risk spending here themselves—and used that to form a layer, like a bed of lettuce, along the bottom of the large zip bag, the kind gym coaches use to carry balls or other equipment. The effect was pretty good. It would pass a quick glance, which was all they needed. At that point, however things went, the count wouldn't matter. Someone would be dead.

Then with a kiss and a "See you later," Heather hopped onto the elevator, carrying a small case with the items they were taking: fake passports, real money, jewelry, toothbrushes, and underwear. She rode down to the parking levels and got in the silver Mercedes she'd decided to steal earlier. It took her less than a minute to disable the alarm and go. She exited, using the card key the owner had left on the dash, turning her face from the cameras. Then she slid into a spot by a hydrant, right beside the entry- and exit-way. She put the car in park but left the engine running. If the cops came she'd smile sweetly and say she was waiting for her husband, and most likely, in her experience, they'd leave her alone.

Then Adrian and his men went down, locking the apartment behind them. They got off on parking level four. Larry took up a position at the curving concrete wall, where he could see down into level three. He assembled his rifle. Next the other two men got in the car, also stolen, that they had left there, a plain four-door Camry, something no one would notice. Curly drove, while Moe sat in the passenger seat, pistol in his lap.

Last, Adrian began walking along the curved ramp, parked cars on either side, descending to level three, where he stopped when he saw a man walking toward him.

"You must be Joe," Adrian said.

46

Joe and Yelena walked from Penn Station to the meeting spot, which was just a few blocks away. As they passed Heather in the silver Mercedes, she thought she recognized them, vaguely, from the park, though it was hard to be sure. As they passed the parking attendant in his booth, Joe waved casually and he waved back. To him they were just another rich couple, a man in a dark suit and a well-dressed, attractive woman, fetching their car or taking the elevators upstairs. But as soon as they had walked up the ramp and out of sight, Yelena took off running. Keeping to the wall, hiding behind cars, she chose a position toward the bottom of level three from which she could cover Joe. She took her rifle from her backpack and waited.

Joe walked at a deliberate pace, hands by his side. He had his handgun, the 9mm Sig, in his waistband and the plastic case in his left side pocket. In his right was an extra loaded clip. As he came up the ramp to level three, he kept his eyes straight ahead, though he knew Yelena was somewhere to his right. Then he saw a man in a black T-shirt and linen walking shorts holding a big zip bag.

"You must be Joe," the man called.

"Hi, Adrian!"

Adrian walked forward a few more paces.

"Hold it, Adrian," Joe called. "Not so close."

"I'm unarmed, Joe," he said. "Look . . ." He dropped the bag and turned, holding his shirt up. "Do you have the item?"

Joe took the plastic case out and showed it. "Can you unzip the bag and show the money?" he asked.

Adrian unzipped the bag and displayed a large green salad.

"Okay," Joe said. "Let's do it."

Adrian zipped the bag and then threw it so that it landed at Joe's feet. Joe grabbed it. Then, underhand, he tossed the case so that it arced high. Adrian caught it, and just at that moment, Joe heard a shot ring out from behind him.

"Sniper!" Yelena yelled as she fired, and Joe dived right. Larry, who had been aiming at Joe, dropped like a shot bird from above and hit the floor with her bullet in him. At the same time, the Camry, which had been moving down the ramp, pulled up alongside Adrian. Curly stepped out behind the open passenger door and opened fire, missing Joe as he landed behind a car, but winging Yelena, who had stood to shoot, exposing herself as a target.

"Fuck," she muttered. Joe crawled over, drawing his gun and firing as Adrian and Curly dashed for cover.

"Bad?" Joe asked her.

"*Nyet,*" she said, and smiled grimly. "Just a grazing."

Still, the bullet had carved a slice from the meat of her arm and the blood was beginning to ooze.

"Here," he said, pulling his tie off and wrapping it tight around her arm. Then he took off his jacket and put it over her shoulders, where it would hide the wound.

"Too bad you did all the dope," she told him.

He laughed. "Sorry about that." He gave her the money bag. "Go find a doctor," he said, and then, before she could say anything, he started to run up the ramp. She fired her whole magazine, trying to give him cover, and then she ran.

Moving up the ramp, with Yelena's bullets streaking over him, Joe saw Adrian running back toward the stairs and took a shot at him, without luck. Curly had taken cover back inside the car, and now that they saw Joe coming toward them, Moe stepped on the gas, flooring it. They could plow over Joe and keep going, making their escape while covering Adrian's as well.

When Joe saw the car coming straight for him, he sped up, reaching the center of level three, where the floor flattened out, and then, facing the oncoming car, he started shooting while running right at it. Shooting while running full speed is less than ideal, so his first shot was a bit high, striking the upper portion of the shatterproof windshield. The next shot was on target, chipping the glass through which Moe was staring back at him, bearing down, but the slug still bounced off, landing somewhere on the ground. The third shot struck just above the chip, and a star appeared. The fourth spidered the windshield. The fifth shattered it, and the glass crumbled onto the dash and onto Curly's and Moe's laps. The sixth shot killed Moe.

As he fired the sixth shot, Joe, who had been running flat out with his right arm extended stiffly and shooting while his left arm pumped, realized that he had only a few feet left to go before the speeding car struck him. There was no time to dive clear now, and nowhere to go, with parked cars on either side. When his sixth bullet hit, exploding Moe's head in a red burst, Joe did the only thing he could think of. He jumped onto the car.

Joe jumped forward, as though in a track meet, leaping up, right leg extended, and coming down with his right foot on the hood of the onrushing car. As it sped beneath him, Joe took another stride, with his left foot now landing on the roof. At this point he stumbled and took another off-kilter stride, his right foot touching down on the trunk, as the car, with the driver dead, veered left. Joe tumbled, ass over head, rolling off the trunk and onto the concrete floor as the vehicle struck a parked car and stopped.

Joe rolled, momentum carrying him over, tightly grasping his gun, and the upward slope of the rising floor stopped him. He jumped up, slightly dizzy, waving his gun while he got his bearings. He saw the Camry, smashed against the parked car, airbags inflated, and started to run toward it, gun pointed.

He came up on the passenger side, since he knew the driver was gone. Curly, banged up but alive, was fighting his airbag and trying desperately to get his seat belt off so that he could get out of the car.

"Glad you wore your belt," Joe said, and shot him behind the ear. He checked quickly for guns, but there was none in sight. No doubt, on impact, they'd bounced around the car and landed out of reach. Joe turned and ran again, this time toward the stairwell where Adrian had gone. He had two bullets left.

47

In the stairwell, Joe heard an alarm squawking and ran up the steps to where an emergency door stood ajar. A security guard was just coming through.

"Thank God," Joe told him. "Sir, we need help. There's been an accident."

"Where?" the guard asked.

"Next level," Joe said, pointing downstairs. As the guard passed him, Joe yanked the Taser from his belt.

"Hey," the guard said, turning toward him, and Joe fired. The jolt knocked the guard back against the wall and he crumpled to the ground. Joe took his hat—a ball cap with SECURITY written on the front—his walkie-talkie, and the little tin badge he had pinned to his shirt. He had no gun.

Joe walked through the door, pulling it shut behind him. The alarm stopped. He spoke into the walkie-talkie: "Level three door secure."

"That you, Tim?" the radio said. "Base to Tim. Over."

"Yeah. Tim to base. All okay," Joe mumbled through his cupped hand into the radio. "Base, my radio is acting up," he added, then threw it into a trash can.

He entered the mall, pinning the badge to his white shirt. There were shops and restaurants and a milling crowd of tourists around him. He tipped his hat to a family. "Howdy, folks."

"How-dee?" the mom replied in a thick German accent.

He continued to move through the crowd, scanning for Adrian. He caught a glimpse of him—black T-shirt, linen shorts—riding the escalator up. Joe started running.

"Security, sorry, security," he said, brushing through shoulders and fanny packs. He pushed his way up the escalator, climbing over bags and strollers. Then Adrian looked back and saw him.

Adrian broke into a run, shoving people aside. A lady in heels toppled as he clambered over her. A man dropped his iced coffee on a kid in a stroller who wailed, while Joe squeezed by as fast as he could. Then, as Adrian reached the top of the escalator, a muscled, inked guy in a T-shirt and shorts felt Adrian push him and pushed back. "Yo, dude!"

Adrian punched Yo Dude in the throat and, as he gurgled, shoved him back down the escalator onto the people behind him. There was a scramble as they struggled with his bulk. Traffic piled up.

Seeing Adrian get off the escalator, and blocked by the crowding above him, Joe jumped onto the barrier that ran between the up and down sides. "Watch out—security!" he called as he climbed up, trying not to step on too many fingers. He hopped onto the moving handrail as he neared the top, riding like a surfer and grabbing a few passing heads for balance, then jumped down onto the next floor. He checked the crowd. A yell and a crash rang out from a dining area. Adrian had knocked over a waiter.

Joe raced after him, hopping over the crouching waiter, who was cleaning up his spilled tray. "Sorry," he said as he banged into a busboy trying to refill some glasses. Ice water tumbled over the table and onto the laps of the guests. Adrian glanced back at him, then cut through the tables and headed across the floor for the elevators. One was arriving. The doors slid open, disgorging a full load of passengers.

Realizing he'd never get through in time, Joe pushed to the head of a long banquet table, full of well-dressed celebrators sharing food and wine. He put one hand on a lady's bare shoulder and another on a man's bald head and vaulted himself onto the table.

"Excuse me," he called as he ran down the table, trying to step lightly, but kicking over plates and glasses. A woman screamed as wine splashed onto her dress. A man's salad was dumped in his lap. Joe leaped right over the elderly gentleman at the end of the table, who was still holding his wineglass up, frozen in shock, mid-toast.

Joe broke into a sprint as he saw Adrian join the crowd of passengers boarding the elevator. Elbows locked like a lineman's, he plowed through the crowd, shoving shoppers, and upon seeing the doors closing, he sprang, arm outstretched, and slid a wrist between them.

From inside the packed elevator, Adrian saw Joe's hand intrude between the doors. He grabbed his fingers and bent them back, trying to break them, while blocking the crowd's view with his body. "I think he's stuck!" he said to the others.

The doors bounced open, and Joe's other fist came through, punching Adrian in the side of the head. He jerked back, still holding Joe's wrist, and mashed into the crowd, while Joe pushed aboard. Now the two men were pressed against each other, held in place by the jam of bodies surrounding them. Joe was squeezed between a heavyset couple in matching shorts and T-shirts with each other's faces on them, a woman with a baby in a sling, a teenage girl with headphones on, and a fashionably dressed young man loaded with shopping bags.

Adrian swiftly punched Joe with an uppercut, knocking the young man's sunglasses off, too. "Hey," the man complained, feeling for the lost glasses.

In return, Joe headbutted Adrian, who rebounded off the teenage girl. Adrian kneed Joe in the groin, and Joe, swiveling to avoid it, knocked into the T-shirt couple, who pushed back as Joe stomped his foot onto Adrian's toes. Adrian kicked Joe in the shin and brought an elbow up. Joe ducked and Adrian's shot glanced off the baby, who began to scream. Afraid that he'd hurt the baby, Joe turned away, and Adrian got a chance to poke him in the eye. Joe winced. Momentarily blinded, he stumbled back as the door opened on the floor above. Passengers spilled out. Blinking his eye clear, Joe saw Adrian hurry down the hall. This was a residential floor with apartments on both sides. A middle-aged Asian lady was unlocking her door while balancing several packages. Adrian pushed her aside and entered the apartment as Joe came running over.

"Security!" he told the stunned woman, and rushed past her, entering her home. He chased Adrian around a long white dining room table and into the all-white living room, where a middle-aged Asian man in sweats was practicing putting on a white carpet. He looked up in shock as Adrian shoved him over and took his club. Adrian swung the club at Joe, whipping it back and forth, while Joe ducked and jumped. Then he smashed it hard into the sliding glass door to the terrace, shattering the glass, and hopped through, hurling the club back at Joe. Joe knocked the club away and pursued him, stepping onto the terrace just in time to see Adrian climb over the partition and onto the neighbor's side. Joe climbed over, too.

The neighbors were having a party. A bunch of kids sat at a long table wearing party hats and blowing kazoos, while parents milled around, drinking beer. A dad worked the grill, flipping burgers, while a mom served them from a platter. There were presents stacked in a corner and a cake to one side. No one moved. The grown-ups stared in shock and the kids in wonder as Adrian ran through the party and then jumped, busting through the bamboo screen that blocked off their view of the neighboring terrace on the other side.

Joe ran after him, yelling, "Security," and bounded onto the next terrace, which was full of plants. He crashed through some potted palms and fell onto a chaise longue, hopping up as Adrian ran through the open door into a bedroom, where a Mediterranean couple were having sex. Eyes shut, clad only in jewelry, the curvy woman was riding the man, bouncing hard and smacking his woolly chest while techno music blared. Her eyes opened just as Joe passed by, and she screamed, screaming even louder when she saw the crowd of kids in party hats watching from the terrace, some still munching on burgers and franks.

Joe chased Adrian through the living room, which was full of modern art, and back out into the hall. Skittering around a corner, he saw him going for the stairs. He ran into the stairwell and heard his steps drumming above him. Adrian was heading up.

48

Yelena ran. After she was hit and Joe bound her arm and left her with the money, she did what she could to help him, emptying her weapon to provide cover. Then, turning to flee, she was stopped in her tracks by the sight of Joe running straight at the car and firing into the windshield. She felt certain she was watching him die. But his next shot killed the driver, and just before getting run down, he leaped onto the hood, scampering over the speeding car, and jumping off the trunk. When the car crashed it seemed to snap her back into reality. She was wounded, soon cops would come, and, for now at least, Joe was alive. So she ran.

She ran down to the street level and then slowed to a casual stroll, Joe's jacket draped over her shoulders, hiding the wound, and the money bag slung as though she'd been shopping. She smiled at the guard and he grinned. Then she cut in front of a parked silver Mercedes and waded into traffic for a cab. She found one, finally, a block later, and, slumping in the back, she gave the driver an address in Brooklyn.

Later, when she'd been fixed up and had a chance to rest, she sorted the money. Some was just scrap paper. Some was counterfeit, decent quality, probably North Korean, and she burned it. The remainder was $50,000. Less the five she owed her Russian contacts for expenses, that came to fifteen each for Juno, her, and Joe, if he survived.

49

Joe reached the roof. He pounded up ten flights after Adrian and pushed through the exit door. At first there was nothing but the vague oceanic roar of wind and city, and a blazing white sun in a blue sky. Gun drawn, he came around to the west side of the building. And there was Adrian, standing by the edge, holding the glass vial out over the railing. The empty plastic case was on the roof before him.

"For fuck's sake, you must be in good shape," Adrian said, catching his breath. "If I live through the next five minutes, I am definitely getting back on the treadmill."

Joe moved closer, slowly, keeping his gun trained on Adrian.

"Hold it right there, Joe," Adrian said, and Joe stopped. "There's something I should explain. This vial, you may be shocked to learn, doesn't really contain perfume."

"I had a feeling."

"I'm told the virus is extremely nasty and spreads very nicely via the air." He glanced over his shoulder at the High Line beneath him. It swarmed with tourists on this sunny day. "So if I drop this, on purpose or because I get shot, well, at first it won't be that bad. Maybe one unlucky soul gets

247

bonked on the head. But within a couple of minutes, I'm told, at least a few dozen will breathe the stuff in. Perhaps many more on a nice breezy day like this. So let's say, to keep the math simple, like fifty? Those fifty will go about their lives—get on the subway, eat in restaurants, go to the movies—and by tomorrow each will breathe on fifty more. By the next day those fifty will each infect fifty, and since so many are tourists, they will get on planes and land in airports all over the country and maybe the world. How many does that come to?"

Joe shook his head. "No idea. I suck at math."

"No doubt. You strike me as a man of action." He waved the vial. "About one hundred twenty-five thousand. How does that sound to you?"

"Extreme."

"Yes, well, I am an extremist, I'll give you that. But considering how many people the United States has killed, or caused to be killed, worldwide, really it is just a beginning. Even this stuff"—he tossed the vial into the air, flipping it like a coin, and caught it—"was made in the good old USA, after all. And the reason there's no cure is that your leaders haven't figured that part out yet, or gotten a chance to see what happens when they drop it on some people with funny-sounding names." He held the vial up proudly, like a prize. "Now how do you feel about your beloved United States of America?"

"Ambivalent," Joe said. Then he fired.

The vial shattered, and Adrian startled as it fell from his hand, down to the crowd below. "Holy shit!" he yelled, peering over. He smiled wildly. "I have to say, I never saw that coming."

Joe kept the gun on him. One more bullet.

Adrian laughed happily. "You were listening to that part about all the dead people?"

"Kind of," Joe said. "But you were so busy talking, I didn't get a chance to tell you. I boiled that vial in the microwave last night for, like, twenty minutes. The most it will do now is maybe stain someone's shirt down there. If you're lucky."

A thoughtful look crossed Adrian's face. Then he laughed, loudly, shaking his head. "But, Joe, why are we even up here then? I mean, if you had the money and you knew the bug was dead, why bother? What do you even want?"

Joe took his phone out and, keeping the gun aimed on Adrian, held the camera up with his injured left hand. "How about a smile?" he asked.

He snapped the picture, and Adrian looked perplexed as Joe selected one of the many missed calls from Gio and pressed send.

Agent Donna Zamora was back in the basement. The investigation was ongoing, as they say, but while the vast machinery of law enforcement ground on, life began returning to normal. And normal for her was at her desk, checking to see if anyone who'd seen anything was saying anything of interest. The answer was not really, but she was enjoying the relative peace for once, when her phone rang. Not the tip line. Her personal cell. An unknown caller. She answered.

"Hello?"

"Hi there, is this Agent Zamora?"

She recognized the voice, the smooth, educated tones, the Queens accent subdued but still potent, like a recessive gene. "Gio?"

"Hold on. I'm sending you a picture."

"What?" she asked him, confused.

A photo icon popped onto her screen and she tapped it. A face appeared. "Is this him?" Gio's voice asked. She was staring at Adrian Kaan, the man her whole office, the CIA, and the local cops were hunting. He appeared to be outside with blue sky behind him. He was smiling, sort of. A sad smile.

"Where did you get this?" she asked.

"Is it him?" Gio repeated. "Yes or no?"

She looked from the phone to the photo on her wall and back. "Yes," she said.

"Thank you," Gio said, and hung up. The picture vanished.

When Heather saw the blond chick from the park go by a second time, but alone now and carrying the money bag, she started to get nervous. When she heard sirens, she knew something was wrong. When she saw cop cars pulling up and being waved into the parking structure by the guard, with an ambulance behind them, she knew: she wasn't going to see her husband again. She put on her turn signal, and a flustered cop waved her along. As a fire truck turned onto the street, she pulled away, waving and smiling thanks at the cop, who waved back.

Driving to the airport, she felt a strange mixture of grief and pride. Her husband was lost to her, but he had died fulfilling his destiny, and she was carrying his child. She put the radio on, waiting to hear the news. She heard nothing.

Even days later, when the virus should have been slaying thousands, she heard nothing, she read nothing. She found a small story on the *Post* website about a robbery in the mall, foiled by a brave security guard, who chased away the bandit. Fortunately, no innocents were hurt. And then, as she lay on the beach, behind her shades, with her microscopic baby growing in her still perfectly flat belly, her feelings changed, and she felt only burning rage and a cool, delicious desire for revenge.

50

The next time Donna heard from Gio, it was the following day, and he called over the office line, patched through from the switchboard. He wanted to meet. She had been thinking about getting some air during her lunch break anyway, so she agreed to meet him by the water, a discreet distance from her office. She was on a bench, finishing her salad, when he appeared.

"Hi," he said, sitting at the other end. "Gorgeous day, isn't it?"

"Pretty good so far," she agreed, and sipped her water.

"The reason I wanted to see you is that I came across this and thought you might be interested." He handed her an object wrapped in a paper towel. It was an artfully produced plastic case of oblong shape with beveled edges and a number on it. She knew the description by heart. But it was empty. "I hear it used to have perfume in it," Gio said, "but that got destroyed. Completely."

"Where did you find this? Who gave it to you?"

"I can't recall," he said. "But I'm told that a cleaning person found it in an apartment overlooking the High Line."

He told her the address and apartment number. She knew that building was being systematically searched, but there were a hundred apartments, plus stores, offices, and so forth.

"That's a funny coincidence," Donna said.

"How so?" Gio asked.

"Adrian Kaan, number one most wanted on the terror watch list? He was found on the roof of that building."

"No shit? Did you get him?" Gio leaned in, smiling innocently.

"Somebody did," Donna said, and touched his forehead. "With a single bullet right between his eyes."

"Nice shot."

"Very nice. And whoever it was left three more terror suspects dead in the parking garage, too. Freed up a lot of space on my wall."

"That's terrific. Sounds like somebody is a very good citizen."

"Well, a very dangerous one at least."

"Speaking of good citizenship," Gio said, removing a cigar from a case in his pocket. "Do you mind?" he asked, pausing. "You're done eating?"

"Go ahead," she said.

"Speaking of citizenship," he repeated, flicking his lighter and puffing, "I admit I came here hoping to ask a favor."

"What a shock."

"Nothing crooked," he said, waving the cigar. "I'd never ask that. I have too much respect for you. It's for a friend. You see, this poor kid, his name was Derek Chen, he was from Queens like me. Anyway, he was killed, tragically, in an incident that I believe you were involved in, too, a robbery at an illegal gun show. Anyway, his family are friends of mine, and I know it would help them to, you know, get some closure, if they could see the official forensic reports, specifically the one showing that the shots that killed him were fired by one of the redneck gun nuts you guys took into custody."

"Why doesn't the family just file a request? Once the case is closed they can get a copy of everything."

"That could take months. Plus all those legal headaches. Like I said, I think seeing that report now, like today, would really speed up the grieving process and let them start healing."

Donna nodded. "I think I can accommodate that."

"Great! Thank you so much," Gio said, and stood up, shaking her hand. "Oh . . ." He paused. "And with so many terrorists eliminated this week, can I tell my friend Mrs. Greenblatt it's okay to open her club? We're off red alert?"

"Yeah." Donna waved him off. "She's back in business."

"Thanks. She'll be thrilled." He turned to go.

"Hey . . ." she called after him. He turned around. "Your pal Joey. Will he be back working there, too?"

"Where else would he be? He's the bouncer."

51

It was a quiet afternoon, still early, and Joe was in a back booth, drinking coffee and reading *The Trial*, by Franz Kafka, when Agent Donna Zamora walked in.

"Hi, Joe."

"Hey!" He smiled and put his book down. The little finger and ring finger of his left hand were taped together. "Have a seat."

"Thanks." She sat across from him.

"You want anything? Drink? Lap dance?"

She smiled and he smiled back, that same gleam in his eyes. "Nah," she said, "I'm driving. And anyway, my chest is a little sore."

"That's too bad."

"Yeah, some bastard shot me with a beanbag gun. But I'll get even."

"I don't doubt it. What about a coffee?"

"Any good?"

"It's strip-club-bar coffee. It tastes like burned shit."

"Maybe later. What happened to your fingers?"

"I caught them in an elevator door."

DAVID GORDON

"Ouch, clumsy. Well, I really just stopped by to say hi . . ."
"That's sweet of you."
". . . and to deliver a friendly message."
He sat back, sipped his coffee, waiting, smiling. She leaned in.
"Your nation owes you a debt of gratitude," she said. "More than it'll ever pay." She paused, but his smile remained unchanged, his eyes on hers. She continued. "But you are a private citizen now, and as much as I might appreciate your unique talents, remember, if you happen to hear about any crimes or possible crimes being committed, just call us and leave it to the professionals, okay?" She looked at him. Her question hung in the silence.
"But I am a professional," he said with a grin, pointing at his T-shirt. "See, it says right here, I'm security."
She laughed, the moment passed, and she stood. "Then I guess I'll be seeing you around, Joe Brody." She put her hand out and he shook it.
"I definitely hope so, Agent Donna Zamora."
Their eyes met once more and then she left. He watched her walk out, and was just getting back to his book, when Kim sauntered up, robe over her sparkling G-string and matching heels.
"Hey, Joe, the manager wants you."
"Right," he said, laying the book down and standing. "Thanks, Kim."
"*The Trial*?" she said, turning her head and reading the upside-down title. "I don't know, Joe, I'd spend the money on a real lawyer, not do it yourself out of a book. Remember my ex-boyfriend?"

"Which one?"

"The jealous asshole crackhead? He tried dealing with the cops on his own, and he ended up in a dumpster. They're still missing some parts."

"Thanks," Joe said, "I'll remember that," and walked back to the manager's office. He knocked.

"Yeah?"

He went in, and when the manager, a retired felon who looked like Santa, but with a boozer's Rudolph nose, saw it was Joe, he just nodded and went back to doing the books. Joe shut the door and then crossed to another door in the opposite wall. He opened that one and exited into a narrow alley, really just an airspace between two buildings, full of cigarette butts and old bird shit, closed off at both ends. He crossed the alley and knocked on a rusty metal door. It swung back, revealing stairs to the basement.

"Hey, Joe," Nero said, and held the door open. "Go right in. They're waiting."

"Thanks, Nero," Joe said, and headed down.

Nero shut the door behind him. The basement was a low-ceilinged, windowless room with cinder block walls and a cracked concrete floor. Weeds sprouted through here and there. In a circle of folding chairs sat the same people who had met with Gio at the salt and sand shed the week before. The one new face had a ring through its nose, a heavyset white guy with a shaved head and a bunch of piercings. He had a small blowtorch lit and was heating a long, narrow bit of metal that he held with a thick glove. Gio saw Joe.

"Here he is, the guest of honor. You ready, Joe?"

"Ready." Joe took off his T-shirt and dropped it onto a chair. Gio gripped him by the right arm. Alonzo, the black gang leader, stepped up and held Joe's left arm in his muscular grip.

He whispered to Joe, "Just want to say thanks, on behalf of Juno's people."

Joe nodded, but before he could speak, Gio put a wooden pencil in his mouth. "Here, bite on this."

The bald, pierced guy walked over, holding the now glowing red brand in his gloved hand. While everyone watched in silence, and Gio and Alonzo held Joe still, he pressed the burning metal into the flesh, high on the left side of Joe's chest, on his pectoral muscle. Joe writhed, moaning, and spit out the pencil. The two men held him tight. Then, while Joe breathed heavily, the guy treated and bandaged his burn.

Gio hugged him, kissing both cheeks. "Congratulations," he said.

Alonzo hugged him, too. Uncle Chen was next.

"I'm sorry about Derek," Joe said. "I can tell you he died fighting, on his feet."

Uncle Chen nodded, then squeezed both of Joe's hands in his.

Next, Menachem the Hasid grabbed Joe by the cheek. "You did it, boychick. We're proud of you," he said, and kissed him.

"Thanks, Rebbe."

"And you!" He grabbed Gio. "Kid, you're a genius." He winked at Alonzo. "Am I right?"

Alonzo grinned and patted Gio's chest. "He's a mother-fucking visionary."

The others all lined up, shaking Joe's hand, or gripping and dapping, or hugging and kissing him, depending on the dictates of their tribe. A few smiled and called him "Sheriff." When the burn healed, a small scar would remain, a brand in the shape of a five-pointed star, to mark who he was among those in that room and to their people. It was a sign for those who could read it. It was a badge.

Acknowledgments

I would like to thank Doug Stewart, the world's best agent, who has stuck by me through thick and thin, and all the great people at Sterling Lord Literistic, especially the intrepid and tireless Szilvia Molnar. I also want to thank Rivka Galchen and William Fitch for their early reading and eternal friendship. I also want to express my thanks to Otto Penzler for his insightful and sharp-eyed editing and for adding my book to such a high, wide, and dazzling shelf; as well as to everyone at the Mysterious Press and Grove Atlantic. And, as always, I would like to express my infinite gratitude to my family for their infinite love and support.